HERE'S WHAT CRITICS ARE SAYING ABOUT ANGIE FOX

"With its sharp, witty writing and unique characters, Angie Fox's contemporary paranormal debut is fabulously fun."
—*Chicago Tribune*

"This rollicking paranormal comedy will appeal to fans of Dakota Cassidy, MaryJanice Davidson, and Tate Hallaway."
—*Booklist*

"A new talent just hit the urban fantasy genre, and she has a genuine gift for creating dangerously hilarious drama."
—*RT Book Reviews*

"Filled with humor, fans will enjoy Angie Fox's lighthearted frolic."
—*Midwest Book Review*

"This book is a pleasure to read. It is fun, humorous, and reminiscent of Charlaine Harris or Kim Harrison's books."
—*Sacramento Book Review*

Night of the Living Demon Slayer

NEW YORK TIMES BESTSELLING AUTHOR

ANGIE FOX

This edition published by arrangement with Moose Island Publishing.

Moose Island Books

First Edition
ISBN-13: 978-1-939661-26-5

Interior format by The Killion Group
http://thekilliongroupinc.com

More Books from Angie Fox

The Accidental Demon Slayer series
The Accidental Demon Slayer
The Dangerous Book for Demon Slayers
A Tale of Two Demon Slayers
The Last of the Demon Slayers
My Big Fat Demon Slayer Wedding
Beverly Hills Demon Slayer
Night of the Living Demon Slayer

The Southern Ghost Hunter series
Southern Spirits
The Skeleton in the Closet
The Haunted Heist

The Monster MASH series
Immortally Yours
Immortally Embraced
Immortally Ever After

Want an email when the next book comes out? Sign up
for Angie's new release alerts at www.angiefox.com.

CHAPTER ONE

"Lookie here," I called as I showed the dragon a large, red, rubber ball. The gangly adolescent was as big as a car and not all that coordinated.

He let out a large *ker-snuffle*, his yellow eyes trained on the prize as his flat pink nose quivered with excitement.

"You want this, don't you?" I teased before tossing the ball. "Fetch!"

The white dragon scrabbled after it in a chorus of nails on concrete, tearing through the witches' courtyard as if my grandma had blasted him with a fireball spell.

"You can do it!" my Jack Russell terrier hollered. "Don't get distracted!"

The dragon's wing clipped a wooden rack loaded down with drying herbs tied together with ribbons. Bunches of rosemary, sage, and yarrow scattered across the yard. He didn't miss a beat.

I cringed, and not because of my klutz of a dragon or my dog who spoke English. Pirate had been talking in real sentences ever since I came into my powers as a demon slayer. No, my stomach crumpled at the way the dragon burst straight across the coven's sacred pool, showering a witch named Frieda with a small tsunami of water.

"Aww...really?" she protested, shaking off her arms. The unexpected wave had flattened her blond bouffant hair and dripped down her black bustier.

I should add that my grandmother's coven of witches also happened to be a Harley-riding biker gang. They'd hit the road more than thirty years ago to avoid a particularly nasty demon. Even after I'd taken care of that problem, the lifestyle had stuck.

"Sorry," I called, wishing I had a towel to give her. "At least he's focused," I added, trying to lighten the mood, neglecting to tell her she had a water lily petal caught in her bangs.

My dog's stubby tail thumped, whipping up a small breeze. "Rookie mistake. It's way too easy to go bonkers over fetch." Pirate was mostly white, with a dollop of brown on his back that wound up his neck and over one eye, hence the name. "*Be* the ball, Flappy!" he hollered. Pirate turned to me. "I taught that dragon everything he knows."

I snorted. "In that case, he should be a whiz at climbing up on tables to sneak pork ribs."

"I have no idea what you mean by that." Pirate blinked up at me with wide, sincere doggie eyes.

Innocent, my foot.

Meanwhile Flappy invaded the garden at the back and started nosing through a leafy green mass of plants that could have only grown in these parts with the aid of copious amounts of magic. He stopped, sneezed, and then kept going.

A gray-haired witch named Ant Eater tossed Frieda a towel. "Go ahead and let the dragon stomp through my lavender," she barked, "as long as he hits your grandma with a wall of water next time."

"Charming." I tried to sound displeased and failed. It would be pretty funny to see.

Ant Eater grinned, her gold tooth glinting in the afternoon sun. "Gertie's had it too easy lately."

"She's earned it," I said. "You too."

The Red Skulls had spent so many years on the run, I wasn't sure if they remembered how to settle down. But the last few months had been a pleasant surprise. My grandma's coven had taken over the Coco Cabana, a 1940s-era motor inn near the California coast. A few charms plus early payments had kept the property owner out on his boat, enjoying his own life for the first time, while the witches made a home.

Bunches of white yarrow tied with hemp rope hung over each door to ward off evil. Enchanted crystals glittered from flowerbeds. A fountain made from broken plant pots trickled water over stones and crystals, down onto the fragrant water lilies that bloomed in the old hotel pool. The motor inn formed a U around a center courtyard that was closed in on the back by a tall fence and a massive wall of ivy. It guaranteed privacy, along with a place to do magic.

And play with dragons.

Pots of lilac, sage, and hibiscus dotted the concrete expanse. Flappy thrust his rear end up into the air as he nosed into a thick leafy grouping of plants along the back wall. He stiffened and let out a triumphant huff.

Pirate stood, his entire body quivering. "He did it!"

Flappy emerged, victorious, his jaws firmly clutching a...oh my. I hated to break it to Pirate, but, "That's not a ball."

The dragon snorted as he lumbered past pots of herbs and puddles of water, his yellow eyes sparkling and his large body quivering with excitement. With a happy grunt, he dropped a hot pink motorcycle helmet at my feet.

Leave it to me to ask the obvious, but, "Why was that in the bush?"

A skinny witch named Edwina strolled past us with spell jars in both hands. "Probably from the party last night."

It had been a doozie. In fact, most of the Red Skulls were still sleeping in. I didn't blame them. Let's just say they made the dandelion wine especially potent on the festival of Lammas, or the late summer harvest. After just half a glass, I'd been more than eager to escape to a spare hotel room with my husband, Dimitri.

I liked how he celebrated even better. Especially when it involved me pressed up against the oak wood door of our room. We'd barely gotten it closed before...

"You with us, demon slayer?" Edwina asked as she handed a jar to Ant Eater for inspection. Edwina nudged the curly-haired witch. "Doesn't look like Lizzie needs this particular spell."

Ant Eater held the jar up to the light. "You didn't add the chipmunk whiskers."

Edwina nodded. "They're so small I needed to get my glasses."

I watched them head off, talking about the intricacies involved in brewing a proper love spell.

I didn't even know chipmunks had whiskers.

Meanwhile, the dragon nosed the discarded bike helmet, rolling it around on the ground.

"Isn't that sweet?" Pirate crooned. "Flappy wants to go for a ride."

I hated to break it to him, but, "Dragons can't ride motorcycles." It was a wonder dogs could. I hadn't known biker dogs existed until we'd hit the road with my grandmother's gang.

"The ball, Flappy," I said, pointing, "right there. By the fence." It lay in the dirt about six feet from where he'd dug the helmet out of the bush—a large, red ball. You couldn't miss it.

The big dragon trundled off.

"It's not his fault he can't see color," my dog pointed out. "Look for something round!" Pirate called.

The dragon broke into a run, flapping his wings. Before I knew it, he'd taken off. He flew over the fence and circled the hotel. So much for staying focused.

"You could try to fetch as well," I suggested to Pirate. It had been his idea to teach the dragon tricks. I didn't know why my dog was outsourcing. "You like bringing me balls and sticks. Maybe you can show Flappy where to look."

Pirate sat down instead. "Ah, well, I fetched me some of those leftover lemon squares when Bob wasn't looking. Now I don't feel so hot." He stood, tail up. "Ohh...look what Flappy has now."

The snaggletoothed beast kicked up a small dust storm as he landed. He let out a happy grunt and began lumbering up to us, his mouth full of a gnarled mass of twigs and cloth and I didn't know what.

"Yuck," I said, even before I realized it was covered in dragon spit. "Flappy, drop it."

The dragon laid it at my feet and I took an instinctive step back. I detected the sharp, musty tang of rotten meat.

A bundle of sticks tied with black twine formed a pentagram. Lashed to the center, a crude human form *squirmed* as if it were alive.

"That's even better than a ball!" Pirate gushed, ready to pounce.

"Not so fast," I said, picking him up.

I glanced around the courtyard. We were pretty much by ourselves.

At best, some poor animal could be trapped in the center of that pentagram. At worst...

I bent down for a closer look. This time, the bundle at my feet appeared dead enough. Maybe I was just tired.

The dragon stood over it, panting and happy. Surely his magical animal instincts would tell him if something were off.

I forced some cheer into my voice. "Did you bring me a prize?" I didn't think dragons were like cats, rewarding their owners with less-than-savory trophies from a kill, but I had no clue what this could be. The witches hadn't put it together. Or at least it didn't look like anything I'd ever seen before.

The body in the center consisted of a head-like knot of burlap with a halo of colorful feathers sewn into the crown. A wad of faded yellow cloth formed the body. Poking from it, gnarled sticks made for crude arms and legs.

A faint crackle arose from it, like branches catching fire.

"Yeah, that's bad," I muttered as the large, tear-shaped emerald at my throat prickled with energy. My husband had gifted me with the stone and its bronze chain when we first met. The necklace was loaded with defensive magic and tended to help me out when I needed it. For the time being, though, it held back. Even my emerald didn't know what to make of this thing.

Frieda had gone inside. She'd probably needed to dry off. Ant Eater and Edwina lingered near the back, under the roof by the vending machines, discussing the table full of spells they'd brewed at the ritual last night. Each recycled jelly jar sparkled with pink and yellow magic meant to dispel the darkness. At this rate, I'd need to borrow one.

Pirate squirmed in my arms, trying to get a better look at the object Flappy found. "You want me to eat it?" he offered. "I'm full, but I can make room, no problem."

"No." In fact, I got the distinct feeling it had been watching us. Two black stones glistened on the head of the doll lashed to the sticks. They seemed to follow my every movement. "Go get Grandma." And then, because I really didn't want him back, "After that, take Flappy to my room and you can both jump on the bed."

Pirate lit up. "Get out of town!" He knew as well as I that I never let Flappy inside, much less near my pillow, much less...never mind.

It was a small price to pay. "See if you can jump as high as the ceiling," I said before I thought better of it.

At least Pirate would be safe.

"Yyyyes!" my dog said, with the joy only animals possess. He ran like greased lightning, Flappy in his wake.

He pawed at room 102. "Lizzie wants you!" he said to Grandma as she opened the door. "It's something smelly!" he added over his shoulder as he dashed down the row of rooms. I'd kept my door propped open for fresh air. Pirate nudged it the rest of the way, dashing in ahead of the dragon.

Grandma stood in the doorway to her room, perplexed. She still wore her leather chaps and a black T-shirt from last night. The words *Kiss My Asphalt* curled in silver across her chest. Her long gray hair tangled around her shoulders, uncombed, and black circles lingered under her eyes. She'd had fun.

"We've got a problem," I called, motioning her over.

She nodded, not questioning.

I stepped back to give her a clear view of the mess on the ground as she approached. "I'm hoping maybe you started flinging some crazy enchantments after I went to bed."

She slowed, her mouth forming a tight line as she studied the mess on the ground. "It's not ours."

"Damn." That's what I was afraid of. Now that I could focus better, I felt a presence radiating from it, a deliberate sense of purpose. "I think it's alive."

"Yes and no," she murmured, crouching down to study it. "The pentagram holds in the power; it neutralizes the threat and keeps it inside." She held a hand over it, as if measuring the magical force it held. "If you touch the doll, all bets are off." She glanced up at me. "How the hell did it get here?"

Her guess was as good as mine. "Flappy fetched it from outside the wall."

Grandma stood, frowning. "That's the only way it could have gotten past our wards."

"He carried it by the sticks." Thank God. I didn't want to think what would have happened if he'd bitten down on it. Or eaten it.

Grandma scrutinized the bundle; she could detect a weakness with eyesight alone.

"It feels...dark," I said. It wasn't just the smell or the way it quivered from the inside. There was something else to it. "I want to take a closer look."

She nodded. "I'll watch over you while you do."

I focused my powers. As a demon slayer, I had the ability to draw closer to evil than most would ever dare. I needed to. I liked it, which was another whole level of danger.

With Grandma standing guard, I let go. I called my demon-slayer energy up from inside until I could feel the hot, churning force radiating up my spine, filling my chest. It built. I opened myself to it and let it flow into my arms. I flexed my fingers and tilted my head as the heat invaded me. I held off, waiting for it to build to a razor-sharp stab of intensity before directing all my energy straight at the bundle of twigs and cloth and feathers. It poured out of me, slamming into the twisted mass of energy surrounding the figure inside the pentagram.

At that moment, I saw with sickening clarity the faint gray mist surrounding it, then deeper, to the shard of darkness roiling, colliding, screaming to escape the doll. It panted and fought, hidden from everyone but me. The blood in my veins went cold. "There's a black soul inside this doll."

Grandma cursed under her breath. "You need to be sure," she warned.

"Believe me, I'd love to be wrong." But I wasn't.

My power excited it, made it call out to me.

Black souls were also known as shadow people, wraiths. These were spiritual remains of the truly wicked, those too stained for salvation, the ones flirting with hell.

My mentor took regular trips to purgatory, trying to redeem the ones he could. I did my best to avoid them.

"Okay, then," Grandma said, thinking. "We have to secure it."

"I'm more interested to learn who broke this one out," I told her. Still, she was right. We needed to deal with it immediately, especially since Flappy had crushed part of the pentagram in his mouth. "I don't think we can fix it," I said, unwilling to touch the pentagram. No telling what other kind of magic it held.

"That pile of sticks could break apart at any time," Grandma said. "We need a trap," she hollered over to Ant Eater. "One of the wood ones, with the runes." She glanced at me, worried. "It's double enchanted. We don't have anything stronger. Haven't had time yet."

"You think it'll work?" I trusted Grandma, even if she did tend toward the kind of loosey-goosey magic that made me sweat.

She gritted her jaw. "It's the best we've got."

Ant Eater opened a cabinet near the spell tables and carefully withdrew a wooden box.

Grandma blew out a hard breath as she ran a hand over the back of her neck. "At least we're building up our supplies. A month ago, we wouldn't have had the time to make and dry a trap like this, and we definitely wouldn't have had a secure place to store it."

"It'll work," I said. I'd counted on the witches often enough to recognize their skill. Besides, it's not like we had a choice.

Ant Eater hurried over with the trap, giving Flappy's prize a second and a third glance as she did. "You need me to call the rest of the coven?" she asked, placing it in Grandma's hands. It hummed with energy.

The box was no bigger than a Chinese take-out container. The witches had carved protective runes into every surface.

Grandma traded a meaningful look with her second in command. "Not yet. Hang tight. I'll need you to watch from a distance. Call the others if we get into trouble. Don't try saving us yourself."

Ant Eater nodded. "Right." She'd been backing Grandma for longer than I'd been alive.

"Thanks," I said to her retreating form. Hopefully I could handle this without backup. All told, I wasn't sure what the witches could do if I screwed up. They might be able to scramble enough power to keep a black soul trapped, but I was the only one who could capture it. Or destroy it.

Grandma opened the box. A blue mist swirled from inside, curling over her fingers. "Looks good from my end."

"Then let's do this," I said, closing in on the doll. The air right around it felt hot, sharp. It settled over me, stinging as if a thousand tiny needles pricked my skin.

The last time I'd touched a black soul, I'd pulled it out of a werewolf's chest and nearly killed him.

This one pounded for release. It was angry. Trapped. Waiting. It needed a place to be; it missed having a body. It would take mine if it could.

I rolled my shoulders, trying to keep them loose. *Focus.*

My palms slicked with sweat. Cautiously, deliberately, I touched my fingers to the cloth, willing myself to stay calm as a tiny, marble-sized knot bubbled to the surface. In a million years, I didn't think I'd ever get used to that feeling.

Now. I tore through the flimsy covering and reached for it.

It skittered sideways.

"Frick." I chased it. For a second I gave in to desperation. I lost control.

But in my job, any loss of focus could be deadly. I forced myself to pull back, all the way out. I held my hands out to my sides. *Not so fast.* It wanted me to make a mistake.

I'd kept the pentagram and the rest of the trap intact. Tearing the cloth helped me get to it, but the move hadn't allowed it to escape.

"You okay?" Grandma asked, her voice even more gravelly than usual.

"Yes." I opened my mind, forcing myself to concentrate on directing my power instead of dwelling on the fear of what would have happened if I hadn't touched this first, if someone non-magical had stumbled across it, if the trap broke, if I let it get away. I braced my hands around it again, brushed the hard knot with my fingers, and gripped it tight, yanking it straight through the cloth.

Holy Hades. It sucked me down. I felt the blackness overtake me, the power of it seep into me. My mind swam.

"Let it go," Grandma ordered.

"I am!" I tried to open my fingers, but they wouldn't move. My head felt like it was stuffed with cotton.

"Lizzie!" She gripped my shoulder. It didn't matter.

It called to me.

Another body. Mine!

It feels so good.

I'm almost in.

I swayed, but managed to stay upright, harnessed by the tight whisper of fear. But that gave it power—my terror, my emotion. I let it go. I let the negativity fall from me as I reared back and hurled the malignant spirit away from the people I loved.

The air crackled as the black soul caught on the witches' wards. A cord of hot, red power zipped down my arm, driving a stinging shock through me as the black soul broke into a million tiny pieces that soared toward the afternoon sun.

As I came back to myself, I felt my palms, hot on the concrete, my knees scraping against the rough path.

Grandma had me by the shoulders. "Damn it, Lizzie. You scared the crap out of me." She gave me a shake. "How are you feeling? What do you need?"

My mouth and throat felt painfully dry. "Nothing." At least I didn't think so. I was covered in a thin layer of grit. "I didn't kill it, did I?"

Truth be told, I had mixed feelings about shadow people. The expedient thing was to eliminate them so they could never attack again. But I also knew a fraction of them could be saved with the right kind of intervention. Who was I to deny any soul that chance?

The lines around Grandma's mouth deepened as she squatted down next to me. "You didn't kill it. Or hurt it when it went to pieces. That's what they look like when they're..." She waved a hand at the sky.

"Free," I finished. Free to evolve if they so choose, to seek the good.

Free to hunt.

Grandma gripped my wrist and helped me up. I didn't need it, but it made her feel better. I winced at my stiff knees and tingling legs and shook them out, trying to get the circulation back. I didn't like the idea of that black soul out in the world, but it was a hundred times worse to have it in a position where it could infect anyone who touched that doll.

I planted my hands on my hips and looked to the sky where it had disappeared. "I just want to know where it came from." Grandma's wards should have kept out anyone who wanted to do us harm. They sure zapped that soul on the way out.

Before she could answer, the back gate banged open. There stood a man in a long leather overcoat with a black Stetson tipped over his eyes.

"Jesus, Mary, Joseph, and the mule." I never thought I'd see *him* again.

Chapter Two

Carpenter strode into the courtyard, his eyes on me. "Where is it?" His steps were measured. His leather duster swirled around his legs. Evan Carpenter was a cutthroat, hard-ass raiser of the dead who had helped me exactly one time before he'd declared himself a loner and refused to work with me again.

I couldn't imagine what he wanted now, but I had a feeling he wouldn't be shy about it. Necromancers were rare. Their magic gave them special powers in the spirit realm. This one was especially powerful.

He hitched a hand over his belt, displaying the ornate bronze clockwork ring on his right hand. "What did your dragon do with my black soul?"

Way to blame it on the dragon. "Why did you have a black soul?" I asked. Offense is the best defense, right?

He stopped right in front of me and stared, as if he couldn't quite believe I'd asked that. "I need your help analyzing it. I had it secure until your dragon swooped down and stole it."

"About that..." I glanced down at the ground, to the broken trap at my feet.

"No." He grabbed it, turning it over in his hands, frantically inspecting it for the lost soul.

"We didn't know it was yours," I said quickly. "We had no idea you were even outside. I had to disable it."

He closed his eyes and pinched his fingers to the bridge of his nose. "I get it. It's fine."

No, it wasn't, but I wasn't particularly interested in pushing the point. "Where did you get that thing anyway?"

He stood slowly. "There's a voodoo bokor down in New Orleans. He's trapping black souls. Hard to know how," he said in that careful, deliberate Louisiana drawl. "He doesn't have powers like yours or mine. I was going to show you the trap I stole, see if you could help me figure out how he snares them. But that ship has sailed."

Indeed.

He stood straighter. "In any case, I need you to come down South with me. Immediately."

"As in right now?" I asked, surprised, and a little galled by his attitude.

His blue eyes blazed hot while the rest of him remained ice cold, controlled. "You do owe me."

Way to bring that up. "I get it."

Carpenter had been invaluable on my last adventure. He'd helped me kill a powerful demon and he'd saved my dog's life. He didn't need to hold it over my head in order to get me to listen. But it did show me just how important this was to him.

"I'm having trouble with the dead in New Orleans," he explained.

That didn't sound good. "I sincerely hope you mean ghosts." I'd met a few over the last year or so and I'd had decent luck. Then again, considering he'd brought along a black soul, odds were this would be a lot stickier. Especially if it was something a necromancer couldn't handle.

"A reanimated alligator," he said, serious as a heart attack.

I snarfed. "You've got to be kidding."

He frowned. "Why would anyone joke about reanimated alligators?"

He had me there.

Carpenter glanced at the increasing number of witches gathering in the courtyard, before drawing me a few more steps away. "The undead reptile is the work of the same bokor who trapped the black soul. His name is Osse Pade. They call him the Alligator Man. The scaly beasts are his personal animal totem. He holds sway over them, you see."

"I think I do," I said, decidedly uncomfortable with the strange and deadly kinds of magic out there, and with what Carpenter might want from me.

He moved in closer, his voice lowering. "Pade has a church on the edge of the bayou. He doesn't associate with anyone outside his circle of followers, but locals say he has powerful magic, that he has a direct line to their ancestors." The necromancer's jaw tightened. "I think he's doing more than talking to poor departed Uncle Freddie. I can feel the kind of power he pulls up. It's dark. And he's done something lately to make it even stronger." Carpenter drew back, glowering. He pulled off his hat and scraped a hand through his spiky brown hair. "Last night, I failed to put down Pade's latest 'experiment.' I need your help to kill it."

I hated to point out the obvious, but, "I'm a demon slayer."

He shook me off. "A black soul is giving the animal life. I can handle the soul itself, but the alligator nearly took my hand off. This is a two-person job."

I understood his point. Still, I had to wonder, "Can't you just get an alligator wrangler?"

He gave me a dry look. "And tell him what? And keep him safe how?" He quirked a brow. "You handle demons. An alligator should be no problem."

Good point. "That's all you want?" In my line of work, things were never that simple.

He ran a hand along the back of his neck. "I was hoping you could help me figure out how they're trapping the souls." He glanced to the sky where the soul had taken off.

"Maybe we can still figure it out." I could at least help him with the alligator. "Although it seems odd. I've heard of voodoo mambos raising the dead." Unlike shambling movie or television zombies, magic-based zombies were real. "But from what I hear, voodoo zombies have no souls or awareness."

"This is more than a mindless, drugged, walking corpse," Carpenter said. "The alligator is alive and aware. I drove a stake through its head and it kept coming at me. I've never seen anything like it." He shook his head. "Osse Pade shouldn't be able to summon a black soul that can keep a beast like that alive."

But he had.

"This is crazy," I mused. Ask me to put a switch star into the forehead of a minion of hell and I was your girl. As for the rest of it—necromancy, dark magic—it was a little out of my league.

"So you'll do it," he said.

"I will." Carpenter had been there for me when I needed him. I glanced over to Grandma, who stood nearby, not even bothering to hide the fact that she'd been listening in. "You're coming with me, right?"

"Wouldn't miss it," she said.

Carpenter held up a hand. "Not a good idea," he said. "I traveled here through the Between Realm."

I'd heard of that. It was a special system of superfast travel open only to those approved by the Department of Intramagical Matters. He was more connected than I'd thought. "I've always wanted to see the Between Realm."

"I'd be glad to show you," the necromancer said, keeping an eye on Grandma. "But this isn't a rave. I can't take you and thirty of your closest friends." He returned his attention to me. "Just you."

Impossible. "I need them."

Now he was starting to get irritated. "This is just a quick trip down and back."

I got that. But my gut told me to keep my team together. "When facing undead reptiles, I find it useful to enlist all the help I can get."

Ant Eater grinned. "Want me to show him what we can do?" she asked, raising a spell jar.

"No," Grandma and I both said at once.

"Let's just settle down," I added, before the necromancer got a taste of a Mind Wiper or a Frozen Underwear spell or whatever else glittered in that jar. I leaned in close to the necromancer. "Humor me on this one. Please."

He let out an undignified huff. "Now I remember why I escaped back down to New Orleans the first chance I got."

"That's the spirit," I told him.

"All right," Grandma said, rubbing her hands together. "Let's start packing up."

"Already taking care of it," Ant Eater said, motioning to the dozen or so witches now scurrying around the courtyard. "I've also got a spot in mind for us to crash once we get down there. My family has a place big enough for the coven."

"Fantastic," I said, surprised by her revelation. "I didn't realize you were from New Orleans."

"Not anymore." She shrugged.

"This could be good," Grandma said, warming to the idea. "Ant Eater's family owns hotels all over the city."

Now that surprised me. I took another look at Ant Eater, the hard-ass champion of beer-can pyramids who couldn't seem to get the garden dirt out from under her fingernails. "You come from money?"

The gold-toothed witch huffed. "Could be why I'm so high maintenance."

Grandma clapped her on the arm. "We don't have to let them know you're in town if you don't want."

"I'm not breathing a word," Ant Eater said, with a touch of sadness. "We'll bunk down in my grandma's old house. It's so haunted, the family pretends it doesn't exist. Nobody's been there since she died in 1962."

"Then it's settled," I told her. We didn't mind fixer-uppers.

"I do have to warn you," Ant Eater said, holding up a finger, "the walls bleed."

"From black magic?" Grandma asked.

"No," Ant Eater said quickly, "angry ghosts."

"That's fine, then," I said. "Let's do it."

Carpenter watched the entire exchange with slack-jawed horror. He'd learn soon enough.

Meanwhile, Pirate scampered up, running so fast that he nearly collided with my leg. "What are you doing here?" I asked. Jumping on my bed should have occupied him longer.

He turned in a circle and sat. "Does this house have a porch big enough for a dragon?"

"That dragon is not making a nest on the porch," Ant Eater barked before I could answer.

Pirate didn't flinch. "Then I'll share my room."

"We'll figure it out," I said. I still couldn't believe we were actually going to do this.

Neither could Carpenter. "I really think you and your friends are overpreparing here."

"You can ride with us," Grandma offered, which I considered rather generous after he'd tried to cut her out.

"On motorcycles," the necromancer drawled, "across country," he added, as if the whole idea were absurd.

Ant Eater grinned and said what we were all thinking. "Sounds great to me."

He crossed his arms over his chest. "I'll stick to the Between Realm." He stopped and thought for a moment. "How long will your way take?"

"Three days," I said. Or we could fly. I really hated to leave the bikes behind, though. They were great for quick escapes. Trouble was, ever since Ant Eater broke up with Sid the fairy, we'd been tossed off the lightning-fast fairy paths.

But Carpenter was already nodding. "Three days actually works. They're having a ceremony for the blood moon. We can neutralize the alligator then. You'll get a chance to see them in action. I'd like your opinion."

"I'll be there," I told him.

He drew a pad out of his pocket and wrote down an address on Royal Street before tearing it off and offering it to me.

He held onto the paper a second too long as I took it.

"My friend's place. Meet me after dusk on Wednesday."

Interesting. I wondered exactly who this friend might be. "I'll be there," I said. And we'd just see what the Big Easy had in store for us.

Chapter Three

The witches didn't waste any time packing. Only instead of prepping for a fast bugout on their Harleys, they began pulling out massive wooden crates. I'd never seen anything like it.

"What are you doing?" I asked Grandma, who had retrieved a clipboard from her room and was busy taking notes.

She glanced up at me. "Advanced logistics," she said, gnawing on the end of her pencil. We both stepped out of the way as Frieda scooted past with a basket full of dried herbs.

Grandma caught the blonde by the arm and pointed to some of the others who were removing stacking trays from the crates. "Pack the active ingredients for the protective spells in a separate box from the troublemaking potions." The setup reminded me of a tricked-out version of the containers I used to pack holiday ornaments. "I don't want our shielding compounds coming into contact with any Light Eater spells. Or worse, the Bat out of Hells."

"I've never heard of that last one," I said. "What does it do?"

Grandma chuckled. "Makes you run like a bat out of, well... you know." She shot me a conspiratorial look. "We got plenty. Want to try one?"

"Not yet," I told her. I wanted to say 'never,' but we both knew better than that.

A furrow formed between Grandma's brows as she flipped the page and looked over the second half of her list. "I can't get over all the stuff we've managed to collect while we've lived here. I swear our stuff is breeding while we're not looking."

In their case, it could be possible.

I just didn't get why they had to pack so much of it. "This is a quick down and back," I reminded her. I was starting to see Carpenter's point. "It's just me and him, going in for one night."

"We like to be prepared," she said, "in case things get sticky." She gave me a wink. "It's what kept us alive for thirty years before you showed up."

I got that. I did. But I also wondered if there was something else behind all this.

It had to be tough to live so long without a permanent home, only to find one and have to leave it so fast. "You have to realize you are coming back," I pointed out.

Grandma leaned in close to me, her gray hair tangling around her shoulders. "This is what we're calling a semi-light bugout." She watched Ant Eater scoop a fish out of the sacred pool with a net. "We only take the magical stuff. Not a lot of personal doodads. No entertainment or fancy clothes."

"Ah, so you mean the dart board and your silver-studded leather chaps," I clarified. The witches hardly lived with excess.

Ant Eater strode up. "I've got the transport set up and cleansed." And by that, she didn't mean with soap and water. The stout witch turned to the group and clapped her hands. "Let's start loading."

"What exactly are you using to haul everything?" I asked. The witches didn't have a truck.

"Don't worry about it," Grandma told me. "Neal is lending us an old school bus."

Great. "We're not going to be conspicuous at all driving into town."

"Hey," she said. The silver eagle ring on her finger glinted in the sun. "We're not trying to sneak. If anything, we're your excuse to get close to that voodoo bokor. You're fleeing the crazy witches and seeking out a whole 'nother brand of odd."

"With any luck, they won't even realize I'm there." I planted my hands on my hips. "Does this mean you're seeing Neal again?" I'd been glad when she dumped him. He was a bad influence.

"Nah," she mused. "You know he can't keep up with me sexually."

"Grandma!" I protested, losing whatever shred of cool I'd managed to drum up. I didn't want to think about her and him...and *ohmygosh*. I could feel the blush creeping up my cheeks.

"It's a part of life, Lizzie," she said, being both annoying and pragmatic at the same time. "And, yes, I'm glad we're taking every shred of magic we can spare. If any of this can help us in New Orleans, I'll consider it a good use of resources. Besides, if everyone does their job, we'll be out of here in an hour."

Impossible.

Then again, I knew better than to use that word around the biker witches.

In any case, "It'll take me that long to go home and pack a duffel bag."

Grandma eyed me, serious as a heart attack. "Then you'd better hop to it, demon slayer."

✝✝✝

While I still couldn't believe Grandma and the gang could pull off a full-fledged breakdown of their headquarters in about the time it took me to watch an episode of *The Walking Dead*, I was careful not to waste any time as I headed back to my condo to grab what I'd need for the road.

Dimitri and I had lived in the cozy, two-story townhouse for—wow—I realized it had been almost a year since we married. Time flies when you're shacking up with a hot griffin.

I grabbed a slice of cold pizza from the fridge. Then I called him on my cell as I headed upstairs to our bedroom.

He answered on the first ring, which was so...Dimitri.

"You miss me already?" he asked.

I'd never get enough of that melodious Greek accent. Or his other attributes.

"Lucky for me I could walk this morning," I said as I reached down to scoop up the gray wool pants he'd discarded outside our bedroom door. He'd tried out a few new tricks last night. With mind-blowing results. "Where did you learn that?"

His voice was rich, full of promise. "You inspire me."

I couldn't help but grin. I sure hoped he wasn't saying that in front of a room full of griffin warriors.

Dimitri was meeting with the griffins at some secret location in Seattle, a place you couldn't reach unless you shifted and flew there. "Are you busy?"

"I haven't gone inside yet. What's up?"

I told him about Carpenter's visit and what the necromancer wanted me to do.

Dimitri let out a low snarl.

"I like this sexy protective thing you have going on, but this should be really simple." I tossed the sheets and covers up over the bed, realized how rumpled it looked, and started over. This time doing it right.

A hard sigh escaped him. "I realize what you were put on this earth to do. It doesn't mean I have to like it when you start wrestling alligators."

"Look at the bright side. Maybe I'll be the one who gets to put my hand down its throat."

"You realize this has the potential to blow up into something completely different, not to mention dangerous? I've got a bad feeling about it." He paused for a long moment. "I just wish I could be there for you."

"You're welcome to come kick butt when you finish there." If I wasn't done already. I picked up his cologne from the dresser. It smelled like him, warm and spicy. I replaced the cap. "Just don't fiddle around too much, comparing wingspans and talking griffin smack."

"We also like to see who can carry a wild bull the farthest. Or a moose. Any horned beast will do."

"Please tell me you're joking."

"You'll never know." Voices sounded on the other line. "Damn. I have to go."

I grabbed my suitcase out of the closet. I hadn't used it since our honeymoon. Hitting the road with the biker witches usually meant packing light, but this time, I could stash a suitcase in Neal's bus. "I expect you to come down to New Orleans as soon as you can so you can show me what I'm missing." Maybe we could take a little vacation afterward.

"It should only be a few days. I love you, Lizzie." He said the last part as if he could somehow make it happen if he wished for it hard enough. "Be careful."

"You got it," I said, trying to lighten the mood. "I love you, too."

After we hung up, I opened my closet and began pulling out clothes for the trip. One good thing about being a Harley-riding demon slayer: the outfits I wore made packing easy. I mean, have you ever tried to wrinkle a pair of skintight leather pants?

I tossed two pairs out onto the bed and added a few skirts, some colorful bustiers, and a pair of super-high-heel leather boots, just in case we did add a vacation to the end. I also zeroed in on two pairs of elbow-length leather gloves that I'd originally bought to be sexy for Dimitri, but now realized would make nice protective accessories.

Yes, I was a planner. And it's not like I wanted to touch anything inside an evil alligator's mouth.

A few jackets and dresses later, I turned to the bed and wondered just where I'd gotten all this stuff.

"I used to travel with a belt full of switch stars and the clothes on my back," I said to no one, because my trusty canine sidekick had made a circle of friends back at the coven house and had opted to stay behind and help Sidecar Bob make lunch-to-go. That meant Pirate would steal slices of ham while Bob made sandwiches.

"You done?" Grandma asked from the bedroom doorway, scaring the bejesus out of me.

"What are you doing here?" I grabbed a stack of undies out of the drawer and shoved them quickly into my suitcase.

She strolled into the bedroom. "You gave me a key," she said, as if it were obvious. "Coven's moving faster than I predicted. Habit, I suppose." She crossed over to the window overlooking the parking lot out front. "I told them I'd hurry you up. They should be right behind me."

"Oh no." I mean, I'd had the witches over for a holiday party once, but I didn't want my neighbors to see the entire coven of biker witches pulling up all at once. And in the middle of an otherwise peaceful Sunday.

"Too late," she said as we heard the rumble of dozens of Harleys.

I cringed, heading back to try to close my suitcase. "It's hard enough hiding a dragon," I said, fighting with the zipper.

Grandma pushed the top down for me. "Loosen your bra straps. Your neighbors can't see Flappy."

I knew that. Non-magical people couldn't see supernatural creatures. But, "Believe me, they do notice things." Like when the dragon started my barbeque pit by snorting fire. Most people have to use lighter fluid and a match. I just look at my barbeque and it flames to life. "I didn't even tell you about the time Flappy and Pirate decided to dig for dinosaur bones near the carport." The neighbors watched what they thought was my ten-pound terrier digging a hole the size of a truck. "They unearthed two azaleas and a palm tree." Pirate had been so proud. The

Home Owners Association had been livid. "I'm still on probation," I told her.

"You need to relax while you can. Live a little. It's just a few bikes," she said as the senior witches began rumbling into the formerly peaceful parking lot. Ant Eater led the way, the wind tossing the fringe on her black leather jacket.

A dozen witches followed her, along with a clattery old school bus painted in a way that would make the Grateful Dead proud, then at least twenty more witches behind it.

"Look at that," Grandma said, proud. "Our recruitment drive at the senior center really paid off. The coven's never been healthier."

I let out a groan as my neighbor Sarayh and her brown poodle, Moxie, rounded the corner and stopped cold.

Dimitri and I were going to have to move for sure.

"Look at the bright side," Grandma said, "at least Pirate's not riding the dragon."

We'd been working on that. Pirate didn't always listen. I scanned the motley crowd and saw my dog snuggled in Bob's sidecar. Sarayh's brand-new Prius shook as Flappy landed on the roof.

That was bound to leave a mark.

The witch driving the bus let out a *honk-ta-da-honk-honk* and I wanted to lock myself into my condo and never leave again.

Briefly, I wondered if I could somehow manage to pretend I didn't know the Red Skulls, but no, that was impossible. Everyone around here had seen Dimitri and me on similar bikes. And they'd run into a few of the witches before, although not like this.

I finished securing my suitcase, gave the bedroom one last quick glance, and began heading out.

"Wait," Grandma said. "Before you do, I need to tell you something."

"Can we do this later?" I really didn't want them to start honking again outside. And if even more of my neighbors started gathering, I'd have to explain some things to them that I really didn't know how to put into words.

For all my demon-slayer bravado, I'd much rather pretend to be a normal girl, at least in public.

But from the look Grandma gave me, I knew this couldn't wait. "I've been thinking a lot. Now, I'm behind you on this mission one hundred percent, but you need to understand. Wicca is light magic," she said, "at least our path is. It leaves room for interpretation and aids you in accessing the higher good." She touched my arm. "Voodoo takes you down a different road. It's fixed. You can't go into it with the same kind of attitude you see from us. Voodoo magic is easy to screw up. You can invite the wrong thing in, and if you do, you can find yourself attached to things that will haunt your children's children."

"Wow. Okay." I hadn't realized it was that different. Maybe it had been naïve, but I'd assumed magic was magic, both light and dark.

Grandma cleared her throat. "If you get into trouble, we'll do our best to help you, but I can't guarantee anything."

I didn't like that at all. "You're scaring me, Grandma."

"Good," she said, serious as a heart attack. "You're used to going in switch stars blazing. You have to operate that way. I understand. But know that we might not always be able to bail you out."

I nodded. Grandma didn't make idle threats. "You think it's going to get that bad."

She didn't hesitate. "Yes."

I sincerely hoped she was wrong.

CHAPTER FOUR

Amazingly enough, our merry band of travelers made it to New Orleans in one piece and on schedule. I must have rubbed off on the biker witches.

We rumbled down Rampart Street, catching the sound of jazz musicians in Armstrong Park. Ant Eater took the lead as we turned right on Bienville, narrowly avoiding the busy French Quarter in favor of a quieter block of connected houses. Heavy iron balconies dripped with plants. Some sported dangling beads and hanging flags.

The house at 313 Burgundy Street stood apart, and not simply because it was one of the only structures that sat back from the main street, refusing to share walls with the others. Aside from the overgrown yard and the reticent placement, it held an explicit heaviness about it, a darkness that wrapped around its windows and barricaded the doors.

We pulled up in front and cut our engines. "Home sweet home," Ant Eater muttered.

Yeek. If she thought that, I needed to start leaving out a few Martha Stewart magazines for her.

A small, overgrown garden surrounded the white stone house, snarled behind a wrought-iron fence. The head of a maniacally laughing cherub topped each post, impaled like a medieval prisoner on a pike. A swirling breeze scattered tiny pink flowers from the tree out front. One caught on my shoulder and I brushed it off.

Pirate wriggled in front of me in his new biker dog motorcycle seat. "I smell ghosts," he said, scrambling to dismount before I unhooked him from his doggie harness. "Wait. What?" he mumbled, forgetting his predicament in a way that only dogs could.

"Settle down, bub." We had to be smart. I didn't want to lose Pirate in a haunted house, at least not until we'd checked the place out.

"Flappy gets to do whatever he wants," Pirate protested, watching the dragon land on the roof of the house. Bats erupted from the chimney.

"Flappy's bad at asking permission."

Grandma removed her helmet, her hair tangling around her head and clinging to her cheeks. "I get the feeling something's watching us."

Nobody argued.

Old-fashioned gaslights flickered along the street. It would be dark soon.

All right. Then we'd be smart about it. "Let's check it out."

If this place was jacked up, we'd find somewhere else to stay. Maybe a hotel, although I shuddered to think of holing up in some sort of high-rise where we didn't have easy access to the bikes. A boutique-style bed-and-breakfast wouldn't be much better. Street parking sucked for fast getaways. This place at least appeared to have a yard in the back. We could line up our rides and be out of there lickety-split.

Grandma heaved herself off her hog, watching the house as if it would reveal its secrets. "I can't put my finger on what it is exactly. Kind of feels like that time Hercules the siren infiltrated the lake hideout in '92. Damn that man and his abs. I never spent so much time treading water."

I stood next to her. "The spooky, 'get out' vibe could be good, as long as we're safe behind it." The private nature of the house would allow us to do our work in peace.

The witches parked their bikes along the street for now and blocked the driveway with the bus.

Eater nodded, grim. "You ready?"

"Yep," I said, my hand settling on my utility belt. It held five switch stars, which were the weapon of choice for demon slayers like me. They were flat, round, and sharper than any blade. The belt also held crystals, a few incantations I'd whipped up myself, and a useless yet unfriendly creature I'd inherited from my great-great-aunt. So far, all Harry did was growl, bite, and refuse to leave the very back pocket of my belt.

"We've got your back," Grandma said as she and a bunch of others took up positions just inside the front garden. Creely handed her a spell jar. I recognized the pink and yellow sparkling liquid inside. It was a spell to banish the darkness.

"You got anything stronger?" I asked.

"Yeah." Grandma grinned, displaying two spell jars tucked into the pockets of her jeans. They swirled with a brackish brown and black sludge.

"I'll take a group and cover the rear of the building," Creely said to Grandma, who nodded.

A couple of tourists wearing beads and carrying green plastic drink cups crossed the street and headed straight for us. "Watch it," I said, nodding in their direction. We didn't need to scare them, or get caught unaware if they turned out to be something other than what they appeared to be.

Frieda raised a glittery pink and yellow spell jar in greeting. "Hiya."

They raised their drinks and I saw the bottom of the long cups were shaped like hand grenades. "Cheers," said a bald guy with a brown goatee.

Huh. I wasn't used to the biker witches blending.

This could be a better place than I'd imagined. Yes, it felt creepy and off, but so far I hadn't picked up the kind of evil that set off my demon-slayer senses. Ever since I'd come into my power I was insanely attracted to anything that could slay me, gut me, or send me straight to hell.

A little more than half the witches took up positions on the back and sides of the house, effectively surrounding it. They weren't taking any chances. Good. I didn't mind going in with them covering me.

I entered the garden and immediately felt a chill whisper along my left side. "We don't mean any harm," I murmured. "In fact, I'm sure Ant Eater is glad to be home."

The biker witch snorted.

The brick path was buckled with age. Moss slickened it.

"Grab the key, will you?" Ant Eater asked. "It's hidden in the naked-lady fountain."

The stone monstrosity rested near the center of the front yard, surrounded by spindly overgrown bushes. A statue of a water nymph rose from the center, her arms raised, her chest thrust out, her nose chipped off. Even so, she looked a lot nicer than the real-life water nymph I'd seen awhile back. That one had sharp teeth.

I approached it cautiously. "I hope the key is still there. Didn't your grandma die in 1962?"

Ant Eater shrugged. "That's not so long ago. Besides, it's enchanted."

I expected leafy sludge at the bottom or maybe a cracked and empty relic. Instead, fresh, clear water glittered in the pool of the fountain. It teemed with goldfish and a silver key lay at the bottom. "Amazing." I grinned despite myself. I'd never get used to this magical world. I reached for the shiny key, and as soon as my fingers closed around it, the goldfish shimmered and morphed into a mass of slithering green frogs. "Ohmygosh!" I jumped back, yanking my hand out and splattering my arms and cheeks with frigid frog-water.

"Ha!" Ant Eater barked. "I love that charm."

My heart hammered in my chest. Not that I'd admit it. "That's not funny."

"Yes, it is," she said, taking the key from my slimy, wet hand. "You screamed like a girl."

"I am a girl," I groused.

She wiped the key on her pants. "Oh, come on," she added when she saw me frowning. "You'd have done it too if you had magic."

"Maybe," I grudgingly admitted. I *had* hit her with a Giggle Bomb. And a particularly festive Harlem Shake spell. Sue me, it was kind of fun to watch the blistery old witch shake her booty.

Right now, we had to stay on our toes. She of all people should know that.

We climbed the front steps to the stone patio. White columns rose up on either side and a rotting wooden porch swing rocked back and forth on its own.

"Now comes the fun part," she said, slipping the key into the lock. The door creaked open and neither one of us moved right away to enter the darkened foyer beyond.

"Grand-mère Chantal?" Ant Eater called, passing over the threshold. "You still around?"

I joined her, my boots echoing off the hardwood.

White sheets cloaked the furniture and the place smelled of mildew, dust, and old wood.

Ant Eater shot me a quick glance. "She and her husband built this place in the late 1800s. After he died, she got into spiritualism."

"You mean like séances?"

"Yeah."

The hair on the back of my neck stood up. The air practically vibrated with energy. "Seems she invited all kinds of things in here."

Ant Eater clicked on her flashlight. "I'm pretty sure one of them killed her."

"Hah," a voice chided behind me. I spun around and saw only the glow of light from the front door and the outline of a hall bench draped in fabric.

Ant Eater's light danced over the ornate velvet curtains. A thick layer of dust clung to the heavy fabric. "Steady."

"I'm fine," I said, drawing a switch star. The weapon warmed in my hands, the blades churning. Although I wasn't sure what good it would do against something that was already dead.

The only sound came from the ticking of the grandfather clock on the wall by the stairs. It didn't do me any good to see the clock face broken and the insides torn out.

The lines on Ant Eater's face deepened as she searched the shadows. She kept a firm grip on the spell jar in her other hand.

Silence settled over us. It was as if we'd entered a tomb. Only the slow, rhythmic ticktock of the broken timepiece cut through the deathlike stillness.

Ant Eater stepped into a parlor on the right. Intricate lavender and gold wallpaper still clung to the walls. She ran her flashlight beam over a pink stone fireplace. Fading sunlight spilled from between heavy silver velvet curtains covering the Palladian windows at the side of the house.

"How did Grand-mère Chantal die?" I asked, breaking the silence.

"Drowned in her bath," she answered simply, continuing back to the dining room. "I hadn't seen her much that year," Ant Eater huffed, "even though she was the only one who hadn't given me hell for quitting college to join up with a coven." A rose glass chandelier dripped with crystals. "You didn't do that in those days. Or ever in my family." Her light danced over the empty table, seeming to look for something. "But Grand-mère? She was different. She understood."

She paused in front of an ornately framed portrait of a raven-haired woman decked out in a white ball gown. A gold plate underneath read Chantal Cerese Le Voux, 1936.

"Could have been an accident," I said. I hated to think of anything terrible happening to this woman.

Ant Eater turned away. "My mother found her. Called me straightaway, even though she wasn't officially talking to me." She winced. "Said something attacked her when she tried to pull Grand-mère out of the tub."

I could swear I saw the diamonds on Grand-mère Chantal's tiara glitter. "Maybe this isn't such a great place to stay," I murmured, studying the portrait of the dead woman. She seemed to be watching me as well.

Ant Eater stood behind me. "Grand-mère loved this house. There's magic in that."

True. As long as we could avoid what had killed her.

We continued on through a small butler's pantry crammed with china and boxes of who-knew-what. A low rattling sound came from the kitchen beyond.

I held my breath as we continued toward it.

We crossed into the 1960s-style kitchen and I realized the sound came from the thick knife block on the Formica countertop. It was as if the knives itched to leave their holders and find themselves buried in something else.

"I think Frieda packed some anti-energy spells," Ant Eater muttered, giving it a wide berth. "We'll try to drain some of the hijinks out of this house."

"Or you could end up ticking it off."

A hot snort sounded behind us and I whirled around.

The dragon hunkered on the patio outside, his pink nose pressed to the glass, his nostrils expanding and contracting as he fogged up the window.

I let out a breath. "Flappy, you just took a year off my life."

The dragon perked up, eager for attention. His head smacked an iron plant hanger near the door, sending it skittering into the yard. "Eeeyow, grable, grable."

Yeah, well, I didn't speak dragon. "Stay out there and do whatever Frieda tells you," I ordered, glad the witches had us surrounded. This place was creeping me out.

When I turned back, Ant Eater was nowhere to be found.

"Wait up," I said, rushing headlong into the shadowy room ahead, walking straight into a life-sized, snarling bear. I gave a startled shout.

"What are you doing?" Ant Eater demanded from behind me.

The bear was a head taller than I, with its claws raised and its teeth bared. Worse, "I swear it wasn't there a second ago."

She treated me to that condescending, hacked-off look that never failed to tick me off. "You saying it walked out in front of you?"

"What if it did?" It sounded ridiculous, but I wasn't going to put anything over on this place.

The biker witch followed me into the room. "Grand-père liked to hunt."

The curtains hung in shreds, some torn completely from their rods. The décor in this room trended toward creepy antique hunting lodge. It appeared as if the stuffed and mounted animals had been here for ages. There was the moose head over the fireplace, the brown bear towering in front of me. All sorts of deer and other Bambi-type heads lined the walls. Large chunks of fur had rotted out and worn away, making the animals appear ghoulish.

Oh, and the wall at the back ran with rusty red stains.

"The walls were bleeding," I said, as if this place weren't creepy enough.

Ant Eater studied the stains. "Yeah, but these bloodstains look old."

I stopped in front of a console table decked out with a stuffed squirrel in a canoe. It was weird. "What if this place is more than haunted? What if these things are alive?"

Ant Eater barked out a laugh. "Now who's crazy, Lizzie?"

"I'm serious," I said, refusing to back down. I'd seen plenty of whacked-out stuff since I'd come into my powers. "And you, where did you go when I first walked in here. I lost all sign of you."

"I fell down a trap door," she said.

I spun to face her. "What?"

She held up her hands. "Just kidding. You really are freaked out." She moved past me, checking out the squirrel in the canoe. "I backtracked to the butler's pantry. Grand-mère always kept unusual ingredients."

Good for her. We had more pressing matters to deal with. Maybe nothing had attacked us yet, but if a spirit had murdered Ant Eater's grandmother, it could be only a matter of time. "It might be luring us in."

The crazy lodge room led us straight back into the foyer and it was all I could do not to walk out that front door.

Ant Eater huffed. "Now you sound like my mother."

The mention of her made me curious as to what sort of woman it took to raise a witch like Ant Eater. "Are you going to call her while you're in town?" I wouldn't mind meeting her.

"No," she shot back.

"Is your mom gone?" I pressed, unable to let it go. Ant Eater was in her seventies, so her mother would be in her nineties at least.

"She's still around."

This could be her last chance.

The older witch shifted at my answering glance. "Believe me, it's a kindness that I don't call her," she said, heading up the stairs.

That made me kind of sad, but I also knew she was done talking about it. At least with me.

"Wait up." I gripped the bannister tight, not at all confident that something wouldn't try to shove me off. A tingling started low in my gut. "It feels darker upstairs."

She slowed at the top, in front of a bedroom with a pink door. "Grand-mère Chantal died in there," Ant Eater said quietly.

"Okay," I said, trying to figure out the best way to handle it. She didn't make a move, so I did. I braced myself as I tried the door.

It was locked.

"The real bad energy's coming from higher up," Ant Eater said low under her breath. "Can you feel it?"

"Yes." I could sense the dark tendrils reaching for us.

Chantal's bedroom felt heavy, but not overtly malicious. The energy coming from above was another story entirely.

Still, we had to be smart. Methodical. "Let's check out the rest of the floor. Then we'll deal with whatever is lurking above us."

We found two open bedrooms on the hallway to the right of the stairs, and another two on the left. They were dusty. Empty. But they held no quivering knife blocks, unexplained sounds, no attack bears. (I'm still standing behind my first impression on that one.)

That left a narrow door at the end of the second-floor hallway. "This is the way up," Ant Eater said.

"Is it an attic?"

"A tower." She opened the squeaking door to reveal a narrow stairwell.

Of course. Why did I expect anything different?

The witch didn't seem all that eager to proceed. I rested a hand on my switch stars. "What do you know about...whatever's up there?"

Her raspy breath filled the space between us. "Not much. It never felt like this before..." She gave an involuntary shudder.

"Before Chantal died?" I finished.

Ant Eater ground her jaw. "Yeah."

I braced myself and started up the steep, narrow stairs. My chest constricted with every step, my footfalls sounded stark and hollow. A ways up, the stairs turned abruptly. I followed them around the corner and stopped. The final three steps led to a wooden door painted over in florid gold.

A distinct presence radiated from the room behind it. It held darkness, power, and something else. Curiosity, perhaps. Then I detected something from the other side that made me even more uncomfortable…a palpable interest, in me.

It felt like an invitation, one I wasn't so eager to accept.

I'd of course check out the room. I'd promised to keep my friends safe. But I would be on guard.

I pushed open the door.

Dust motes swirled in the circular room, in the light filtering in from tall, dirty windows at the back. Framed ink drawings of a palm, an owl, and an anatomically correct human heart hung in carved wood frames against ornate gold and mauve wallpaper. A crystal ball nestled in velvet atop a small table near the door.

The circular chandelier held a dozen black wax candles, twisted in cobwebs, their wicks dusty and dark.

A rich gold-tasseled cloth draped over a sturdy round wood table at the center of the room. Two chairs, nice enough for any dining room, stood across from each other.

As I drew closer, I saw an old Victorian-style Ouija board. An ink-drawn eye dominated the center of the board, with rays streaming down to ornate black letters laid out across the faded yellow background. A triangular-shaped pointer lay on top. It had a see-through crystal at the center.

Ant Eater caught me checking it out. "That's a planchette. You touch it and it moves. It's supposed to spell things out."

"Do you believe?" I asked.

She huffed. "I know enough to stay the hell away."

Just then, the planchette vibrated.

"You see that?" I hissed.

Ant Eater nodded, refusing to take her eyes off it.

I drew in a sharp breath as the planchette slowly skittered across the board on its own and landed on the letter *L*.

"Could be just a coincidence," I said, almost to myself. But the pointer wasn't done. It moved again, faster this time, just a few letters to the left, and settled on the *I*. Ant Eater and I shared a glance. It shot down and to the right, to the bottom row of letters, landing on *Z*, spinning, landing on Z again. I glanced to the door and found it open, as we'd left it. That was the only thing that kept me from bolting.

Yes, I'd faced down demons and imps and all manner of creatures that went bump in the night, but I had no idea what this was or what it could possibly want.

It spelled the rest of my name with startling efficiency, and then zipped to the lower left portion of the board and settled on a word: *Hello*.

"Goodbye." I stepped back. I didn't have time for séance rooms or Ouija boards or whatever spirits may haunt this place. We were here to bunk over for as long as it took to rid New Orleans of an alligator with a black soul.

"Wait," Ant Eater pressed. "What if it's my grandma?"

"Is it?" I had to think she'd be less creepy about this.

"Are you Grand-mère Chantal?" Ant Eater asked.

The planchette didn't move.

"You say it," she prodded.

"I already spoke to it once," I said. I'd opened communication in a way that wasn't safe or prudent. "Do you really think it's a good idea to start addressing this thing?"

Ant Eater cringed, but held firm. "I have to know, Lizzie."

This was her family we were talking about. "Okay." I gathered up my courage. It's not like I was a special snowflake. If the board didn't answer Ant Eater, it probably wouldn't listen to me, either. "Are you Grand-mère Chantal?" I asked.

The planchette quivered and slid diagonally, across to the complete opposite side of the board, and rested on the word *No*.

Ant Eater appeared as stricken as I felt. "We're sealing off this part of the house," she muttered.

"Good idea," I said, heading out the door.

She beat me to it, but not before I saw the planchette slide straight down the board. *Goodbye.*

That's right. Goodbye forever. I closed the door.

"Give me some space," Ant Eater said as we crowded together on the narrow stairs outside. She reached down into her bra and pulled out a wriggling black spell.

I slipped behind her, down a few stairs. "You come prepared."

"You wouldn't believe the number of high-power protection spells we packed," she said, releasing it. It sprouted a thin set of wings and fluttered to rest on the aged wood. "It may look pretty, but we brewed it potent. This type acts as a barrier as well."

The witch held her hands out and lowered her head slightly, although I could tell she kept her eyes on that door.

Darkness, danger, black as night. Be ye blocked by witches' light.

Her fingers shook as the spell split lengthwise and released a million little specks of light. They filled the space between her and the door, bursting over it.

Coven strong and power bright.

The hinges of the golden door rattled as the glittering spell pressed over it, winding into the cracks and through the narrow keyhole, fusing it with pure energy.

Keep thee out of mine own sight.

The hinges of the door came to rest, and I felt a lightening of the darkness in the stairwell, as if the spell had blocked whatever lay beyond and sopped up some of the negative energy already in the air.

"How long will it hold?" I asked.

Ant Eater backed down a step, then another, her eyes fixed on her handiwork. "Months, years. Just to be safe, we'll check it every day we're here. No sense getting cocky."

"You spoke in English," I said. Usually, the witches did their spell work in a language I didn't understand.

"Felt right," she said simply.

"Okay." I caught a glimmer of the spell in the keyhole and braced myself in case it didn't take. But the door remained quiet, the hallway less dark.

We eased down the steps, all the while sneaking glances back at the door.

"How did it know me?" I asked. I couldn't recall Ant Eater addressing me by name as we searched the house.

She leaned heavily on the bannister. "Powerful spirits don't need to be introduced," she said, shooting me a worried glance, "they just need you to acknowledge them."

And I had.

She shook her head, resigned. "Don't worry about it. Nothing to do now. We'll keep an eye on it."

"Right," I said as we closed the door at the bottom of the stairs. I hoped it would be enough.

CHAPTER FIVE

Ant Eater stood at the front door. "Come on in!"

It didn't take much more than that. Biker witches barreled up the front. In fact, I hoped some of the tourists outside, with their drinks-to-go, hadn't heard.

Grandma was the first inside. "All clear?" She paused. "It still feels a little off in here."

"Yeah," Ant Eater agreed. "We'll need some Dispel the Darkness spells, a few jars of Anti-Energy in the kitchen and the lodge room. Sage in all the corners..." she said, as if she were making a mental list.

She left out all the details. "There's a trembling knife block, evidence of bleeding walls." Grandma took my revelations in stride until I added, "There's also a spirit in the tower room who knew my name."

"I sealed it in," Ant Eater added. "Could even be good camouflage. Nobody will want to mess with this house."

Grandma nodded. "Show me." I started for the stairs and she grabbed my arm. "Not you. You stay away from it, you hear?"

Ant Eater nodded as she popped the gum in her mouth and started chewing. "Come on."

"Frieda, come with us." She turned to the skinny witch, who'd whipped the cover off the settee near the front door. "Edwina, take a crew and set up wards outside. Creely," she added, pointing to the engineering witch. You couldn't miss her. She had Kool-Aid-red streaks in her ponytail.

"See if you can't rig up an escape hatch through the backyard fence. Something subtle."

I barked out a laugh. Subtle? The Red Skulls couldn't even ride down the street without it feeling like a parade.

Grandma leaned close to Creely. "Set up a hatch that gets us out, but don't let nothing we don't want inside. We need all the bikes secure in the back tonight."

"You got it." The engineering witch nodded.

The sun was starting to go down. That was my cue. "I told Carpenter I'd meet him when dark hit," I said to Grandma, "unless you need me here."

She drew off her leather jacket, exposing the sagging tattoo of a phoenix on her arm. "You've done plenty already. We got this next part handled." She tossed her jacket onto the settee.

Good. And if I could solve the alligator problem tonight, maybe we wouldn't have use for Creely's escape door. Or Grandma's work to reinforce the tower, or any of it.

I could say goodbye to that spirit in the tower before it barely had a chance to say hello.

Grandma drew an arm around me as she walked me out to the porch. "Be careful," she warned, giving me a tight squeeze.

I pulled away. "Come on now." I gave her a quick smile. "It's me."

Her voice drifted over the garden as I strolled out into the dark. "That's what I'm afraid of."

I shook her off, although she had a point. I'd always been the focused one, the planner. In the beginning, I thought that would keep me out of trouble. Now I realized it usually helped me find more.

Nothing to do about it now.

I hitched myself onto my bike, rolled the throttle and punched the ignition. Couldn't resist it. I let myself have a little fun as I steered out into the street, reveling in the warm evening air against my skin. It felt good to get out of that house. It wasn't just the haunting. Something about that place didn't sit right. I couldn't escape the feeling that I was being watched.

Voices, music, and laughter clattered all around as I made my way through the crowded streets of the French Quarter, past bars, souvenir shops, and packed restaurants. I figured the address Carpenter scrawled out for me would lead to a bar or an apartment, maybe a safe house. Instead, I found myself a few streets beyond the emerging nightlife and in front of a voodoo shop on Royal.

Skeletons played cards in the display window, amid stacked displays of good-fortune charms, Lucky Cat candles, and Heat Up The Bedroom linen mist. To celebrate after you won big at gambling, I supposed.

A metal, industrial sign over the door read *Voodoo Works*.

The teardrop emerald at my neck warmed as I pushed my way inside the door. Flower petals and dirt sprinkled down from a green scarf bundled close to the vintage tin ceiling.

A caramel-skinned woman scooted around the counter. "Welcome," she said, pressing her hands to the skirt of her colorful orange and yellow dress, "how can I help you?"

I decided to take a chance. "I'm meeting a friend here," I told her, casually checking out a display of Wash Yourself Clean soaps.

"Carpenter," she said, lowering her voice, even though we were the only ones in the store. "He's in the back. I'll go get him." She began to leave and then paused, her bracelets jangling as she smoothed back her thick, black hair. "Thank you for your help with this."

"You know?" That surprised me. The necromancer had never struck me as one who would trust easily.

She wet her lips, nervous. "I've been watching Osse Pade. He has a business just down the street. Voodoo can be so beautiful, but he has taken a dark path."

She disappeared behind the green and gold curtain at the back, and soon after, Carpenter emerged, tucking something into his pocket. He carried a small sack over his shoulder and a dagger in his hand. "You're late."

"Sun's not down yet." That was the deal. "And why are you sharing our business with the voodoo community at large?"

He tightened his grip on the sack. "It's just Aimee, and she's the one who tuned me into Osse Pade in the first place." He kept walking, as if he expected me to join him. "If anything happens to me, go to her. She can tell you what to do."

I took a quick glance back at the woman in question. She peeked out from behind the stockroom curtain as we made our way to the door. "She doesn't look like much of a warrior."

Carpenter gave me a long look. "Neither did you when I first saw you."

That showed what kind of taste he had.

The necromancer stopped in front of an old brown Mustang parked out front of the shop. It had a bad paint job and a dented side door. "Let's go."

I stopped short. "If you don't mind, I have my own ride." I preferred the control.

"Suit yourself," he said, sliding in the driver's side and starting it up.

I headed to my bike across the street and saw Aimee watching out the window of the voodoo shop. She gave me a small wave, and I nodded back. At least someone knew where we'd be tonight.

The engine on Carpenter's car whined and clacked as it tried to turn over.

Just when I was wondering how he'd fit on the back of my bike, his engine caught and the Mustang pulled out.

Good. I followed him close and tried to breathe through the caustic smoke coming out of his tailpipe. He really needed to get that car checked out.

The sun slipped below the horizon as I trailed the necromancer past the city limits and the levees, to where the houses grew sparse and the dirt roads skirted the swamps.

Insects screamed in the night, mixed with the croaks of bullfrogs. Gnarled trunks of cypress trees rose from the wetlands, their canopies dripping mossy leaves and tangling vines. More than once my headlights caught the reflective eyes of gators on the banks. I watched one turn and slip back into the water, ripples echoing out behind him.

Carpenter's car bounced and jostled like he had no suspension at all.

His taillights flared red as he slowed. I stayed close behind as he pulled off onto a road I hadn't noticed among the trees and the underbrush. It was a wonder the old Mustang even made it past the low-hanging branches. I drew my arms in close to my sides, glad for the leather riding jacket protecting my shoulders.

He stopped amid the tangle of trees, his headlights illuminating a rickety old dock. A small motorboat bobbed in the bayou.

I parked my bike facing the main road then went to join Carpenter, who had busied himself untying the boat. I tried to ignore the way my boots sank into the spongy earth. "Seems I'm going to have to accept a ride from you after all."

He glanced up at me. "Just don't fall out."

"I make no guarantees," I said as he held the boat steady enough for me to climb in.

He tossed the rope in between us and settled in the back where the engine was. I barely heard the hum of it over the sounds of the night as we took off into the heart of the swamp.

His cloth bag lay at my feet. I nudged it with one boot, listening to something rattle against the metal underbelly of the boat. "What did you bring?"

I was smart enough not to open it. It could be magic relics or a powerful talisman.

"Alligator tranquilizer," he said as I ducked under a low branch.

"Let's hope it works." I was up for anything that would make this go quicker.

It would be easy for a person to get lost out here, but the necromancer seemed to know the way. We passed a rickety old house at the edge of the swamp.

"That your summer home?" I teased.

He snorted. "Moonshine shack."

He weaved in and out of a maze of narrow tributaries. I kept careful track of them all.

"Here," he said as we reached what appeared to be an island in the abyss.

He cut the engine and we coasted the rest of the way there.

"We get in, we get right out," he said as the front of the boat bumped the muddy shore.

"Don't jinx us." I helped him drag it up onto the bank, my boots sinking in the muck. I took my long leather gloves from my coat pocket and left the jacket in the boat.

"Stay close," he said, drawing his knife. "There are booby traps in this swamp as well as the odd pocket of quicksand."

I nodded, drawing on the gloves.

We set off through a break in the trees. "You come here much?" I asked, mirroring his steps through what appeared to be the only dry ground in a maze of marshland.

"Only when I have to," he said, sidestepping a gator. The thing opened its jaws and appeared ready to strike. I drew a switch star.

"Watch it," I warned.

He barely broke his stride. "It's not the one we want."

"Oh, well, in that case, let's not worry about it," I mused.

I followed him for several minutes, careful to skirt as much wildlife as I could, as we drew deeper and deeper into the swamp. Insects buzzed around my ears and my black leather pants and bustier dampened with sweat. If we didn't take care of this problem tonight, I was going to start shopping for something else to wear down here.

Carpenter drew up short and pointed to an area dead ahead.

The protective emerald at my throat began to hum. That was never a good sign. It was infused with ancient griffin magic and set to help protect me under threat. The bronze chain thickened and I braced myself for the slide of warm metal against my skin.

I stood motionless as the liquid bronze slid down my torso, over my hip, reforming into—what? It had made itself into a breastplate right before I'd had a shotgun pulled on me. It became a metal helmet a moment before I'd almost gotten brained with a sword. I cringed to think what I needed now. I closed my eyes and wished for a big alligator cage with thick bars and maybe a nice pointy fence around it.

Instead, the enchanted metal wrapped around my calf under my pants and boot, molding to my skin and cooling into what felt like an emerald-studded shin-guard.

I spotted light through the branches up ahead. Torches. I strained my neck to see around the wide bottoms of the trunks and saw some sort of shrine at the center. Movement flickered through the trees. Men.

"You didn't mention any guards," I murmured to the necromancer.

He tensed beside me. "There weren't any before."

Thick candles flickered in glass jars. They formed a circle around an immense white alligator resting on a blood-red pillow. Its fat legs thrust out to the sides and its jaw rested on a large gold tassel at the edge.

"I've got this." Carpenter slipped off the path and into the water. He moved silently through the marsh until he blended into the shadows. I didn't follow. I studied the scene and spotted the necromancer's target. A beefy guard flicked a cigarette out into the marsh. He wore tribal tattoos on his face and arms, along with a necklace of feathers.

The guard held a chain in his other hand. It led to a thick collar around the reptile's neck. He approached the gator, winding the chain around his palm, as if reeling in the beast.

The man turned at a sound from the trees behind him. "Brother Rebe?" he called.

No response.

I had a feeling Brother Rebe had met a necromancer.

I felt a nudge against my shin and turned to see a flash of alligator jaws. Sweet Jesus. I drew back as it clamped down on my shin. The guard yelled. I thrashed, my stomach going hollow as the gator dragged me down into the water. I drew a switch star, the blades on the flat disk churning the moment my fingers wound through the grips on the side. I slammed it directly down onto the gator's wide head.

It let out a grunt, its jaws slackening. I shoved it back down into the water as my free foot touched down on the muddy bottom. The gator sank into the warmth of the bayou as I worked hard to hightail it the other way. My fingers clutched the muddy bank, my weapons hand ready to strike again.

When I sloshed out of the water, I saw Carpenter several feet away on his knees. The guard stood behind him, digging a chain under the necromancer's throat. He thrust out a foot and the white alligator snapped at it.

"Attack!" the guard hollered, straining to finish the job on the necromancer. "Enemies on the island! Attack!"

I fired a warning shot and the guard dropped the chain. The tank of a man stumbled backward as Carpenter turned in one fluid movement to pounce on him, rolling to get his hands around the man's neck.

The switch star boomeranged back to me and I caught it right as the newly freed white alligator rushed me. Damn, it moved fast, hissing the whole way. I might not want to kill a guard, but I sure as hell had no trouble blasting an already dead beast. I aimed and hit it in the forehead with a switch star, watching the blade burn through skin and bone, sinking deep.

The alligator shuddered, its legs stiffening as its momentum carried it another several inches until it came to a rest at my feet. Dead.

"Okay, good." I huffed. That was easier than I thought. I drew off my soaked leather gloves and stuffed them into my belt.

Now we just had to get out of here.

Drums beat in the distance. It sounded like the entire voodoo congregation had heard the guard's cries, and it wouldn't take them long to get here.

"We gotta go," I said, keeping an eye on the alligator, skirting around the corpse and stomping over the red pillow to see how I could help Carpenter.

I saw the marks in the dirt where he'd fought, but the necromancer himself was nowhere to be found.

Oh, geez. "Carpenter?" I hissed, although heck, they already knew our location. We had to run. "Carpenter!" I said a little louder.

I followed the scuff marks and broken branches. Blood spattered the ground, along with sticky-sweet-smelling purple flowers. I picked up a handful and shoved it in my pocket, trying to see through the dark.

With every movement, every word, I was betraying my location to people who very well might want to kill me. "Carpenter?"

I stiffened as a low hiss erupted behind me.

My breath sounded shallow even in my own ears as I turned and faced a very alive, very ticked white alligator. The switch-star hole in its forehead smoked and oozed with thick, black blood.

Oh, frick. "You won't even stay dead for a demon slayer."

The undead alligator rushed me. I hit it with another switch star in the same spot, hoping to at least slow it down. This one glanced off the wound and ricocheted into the trees beyond.

The reptile clamped its jaws on the same fricking leg the other one had. Teeth met metal, the shock of the impact driving through me as I hit it with a switch star to the neck. It let out a high-pitched squeal and clamped down harder.

It twisted its head, knocking me to the ground. Then it was on top of me, jaws in my face. I grabbed hold of its mouth, like I'd seen them do in the roadside gator shows. These suckers had crushing bites, but the muscles that opened their jaws were weak. I held its mouth open, right over my chin, but I couldn't keep it up for long.

Then I felt it. The dark soul calling to me. The animal bucked, thrashing against my side. It began to climb directly onto me, crushing me with its weight as the dark soul inched up its chest and into the back of its throat.

Now or never.

I braced the jaws with one arm, knowing they would snap shut at any second. With my other hand, I reached right through the soft skin of its neck. The black soul nestled like an ugly black marble. I closed my fingers around it and yanked it out.

"Mine, mine, mine." It seethed. It struggled to bury itself in my skin. It wanted inside me.

The reptile had gone limp. I shoved it away, struggling to my knees as I hurled the black soul across the bayou. Birds erupted from the trees as it broke into dozens of blackened shards and escaped out into the night.

The alligator lay gray and dead at my feet.

Holy Hades. I'd let loose another black soul out into the world. Carpenter would have some more cleanup to do, but at least the voodoo cult wouldn't be able to get it back.

I'd done my job. I'd rid them of their prize. Now I just had to worry about finding the necromancer. And more. I stiffened as I saw lit torches in the distance, heading straight for me.

CHAPTER SIX

The torches drew nearer. I braced myself, focusing my strength and my will. No getting around it, I was rusty when it came to the power of levitation. It was the one ability I'd never felt comfortable with and, as a result, had never truly mastered. My stomach felt heavy and my toes tingled as my feet lifted from the ground.

Ignore the wobble.

I rose as quickly as I dared. I had to escape and get my bearings.

Shaking, I grabbed hold of a thick tree branch twenty feet up and managed to swing a leg over the rough bark. It wasn't pretty, but I was up there. The branch crackled under my weight and my heart gave a jolt. Maybe I was too used to falling out of trees during levitation training.

There wasn't much time to dwell. I sucked in a breath as four shirtless men charged into the clearing, carrying torches and machetes. Red and yellow paint streaked their faces and bodies.

The leader wore a thick stripe of purple down the bridge of his nose. He skirted the body of the fallen alligator, his breath coming in harsh pants. A charm made of bones and feathers slapped against his chest. "Brother Bode said he saw a woman. Spread out and search."

I clung to my tree branch, trapped, hoping to Hades none of them thought to look up.

One of the men passed directly under me. He stopped at the watery edge where I'd killed the alligator. "I smell death."

Who were these guys?

I strained my neck to see out past where they'd come. Thick foliage blocked much of my view, but I could make out enough. I clutched the bark in shock when I realized Carpenter hadn't simply led me to an isolated island on the bayou. Darkness stretched past the clearing below, but not far beyond it, a massive circle of torches blazed.

If that was the Alligator Man's congregation, we'd parked ourselves right in their backyard.

The men below me moved with ease as if they knew this part of the swamp well. Voices drifted up from the dark. "I have his boat."

"Leave it," the man with the bone necklace ordered. "We already have him."

Oh geez. They stopped directly below my tree, circling together as they planned.

"I see no girl."

"Perhaps Brother Bode saw a spirit."

Drums began a hard, steady beat in the large clearing ahead. Voices echoed over the bayou, in a French dialect I'd never heard.

"Come. It has begun. The ceremony is more important."

"The girl?"

"If she indeed exists in the mortal plane, she is of no use to us. We have the necromancer."

The leader stalked toward the massive circle of torches beyond the trees, toward the hard beating of the drums. All but one followed. The last man paused over the dead alligator. "Shall we take the vessel?"

The man in the bone necklace turned. "No. Give it back to the earth. It has served its purpose."

He took a long look over the clearing before he led them away. I counted four as they retreated and kept an eye on them until I could only make out torches and not people.

The biker witches would have held back one or two witches, just in case. I didn't trust these people to do any different. Unless I really didn't matter to the church.

"Ha," I said under my breath. Let them count me out. They'd realize their mistake soon enough.

As long as I didn't fall out of this tree.

I drew upon my power and jumped, levitating just enough to make it to a thick branch high on the other side of the clearing. I landed with a thud, my palms burning as they scraped against bark. I winced. It was better than taking my chances on the ground.

I leapt two more trees until I reached a small land bridge over the bayou. It was too far to jump, so I lowered myself carefully down onto the marshy ground and crouched low.

Aye-yay-yay! voices shouted from a large clearing ahead.

The drums beat louder.

I rushed across the wide-open space, ignoring the insects buzzing around my head and the aching in my bones. My boots splashed in puddles and sank down into the muck. I was sweating like a pig. My heart pounded as hard as the drums. I blinked in relief when I reached the trees beyond, kind of amazed I'd pulled it off. Still, I couldn't shake the unsettled feeling in my gut.

Perhaps the biker witches had rubbed off on me because I found myself preferring an all-out fight to all this sneaking around. I drew closer, careful to keep an eye out for the guards, and saw women in white dresses twirling and dancing in front of an immense bonfire. Painted, shirtless men, their backs shining with sweat, joined them, thrusting their bodies in a primitive dance.

A well-built man stood just beyond, his arms raised high. White body paint, drawn to resemble a skeleton, caked his chest and formed a macabre image of a skull on his face. "We beseech the loa! Come to us!" The music changed. The drums stuttered out a staccato beat and the people screamed with abandon, thrashing their bodies.

I'd be willing to bet I'd found Osse Pade, voodoo bokor.

The crowd had spread. A man near the fire spun in a circle. He pulled a knife from the waistband of his jeans and, grinning to the heavens, he slashed the blade across his belly.

"Holy..." I uttered, unable to turn away. Somebody had to help him. Others saw. They had to. He'd sliced deep. Only the wound didn't bleed.

The crowd cheered.

I wiped the sweat from my forehead, not sure what to make of it.

A woman crouched near the bonfire and drew a heated poker. She smiled broadly, dancing with the scalding hot metal like she held a party balloon. I wanted to peel the sharpened rod of metal from her hand, to order her to drop it and back away. It glowed at the tip as she brought that burning edge down hard on her tongue. She did it again and again, and she didn't burn. Her tongue remained pink and whole.

Impossible.

Yes, I'd seen group magic before, but not like this. I didn't know what to make of the crowd or their worship or...oh my God. There was Carpenter.

Guards held him on both sides and dragged him to the center of the crowd. The necromancer struggled, bare-chested and hands behind his back. Black tattoos wound over his skin. He'd been gagged and beaten. The bokor laughed heartily; his long face held serenity and delight. He raised a gnarled stick with beads and feathers and an honest-to-God human skull on top. The priest began shouting something I couldn't decipher while his men tied Carpenter to the pole near the fire. I didn't even want to think of them burning him.

But I wouldn't put it past them.

I needed to do something. Fast. So far, the priest had brought an alligator back to life, which was wrong on about a hundred different levels, but it didn't deserve a death sentence. He'd tangled with black souls, but could I kill him for that? And what about his followers? Men, women, white, black, Asian, and all races in between. They looked like people I'd stumble upon on the streets of New Orleans. Save the wild dancing and the paint. Just because they'd taken part in this gathering didn't mean they couldn't be redeemed. At least I didn't think so.

If I could only get closer…

I inched around the outside of the circle, still hidden by the trees. I was so focused on Carpenter that I almost stumbled over a burly guard before I saw him. Thank heaven he was distracted, entranced by the ceremony.

I'd have to sneak around the other way.

The woman who had been dancing with the poker raised her hands in front of the fire. "Blood sacrifice to the loa!"

Pade held aloft a live chicken and made a great show of it, his muscular arms stretching high, spinning his body several times to display the squawking, frightened bird. The congregants pressed close, turning their faces up in rapture as feathers floated down to catch their cheeks and eyelashes.

With a knowing smile, he thrust the bird to the ground in front of Carpenter, who struggled, his hands lashed behind his back, his neck and feet bound to the pole.

The voodoo priest pointed his skull stick at the bird. He grinned manically as the animal let out a piercing squawk. Blood bubbled up from its chest, without him touching it, without him doing a thing except pointing that cursed stick. Church members collapsed to the ground, kicking and flailing as the bird thrashed, crying out as its blood splattered the congregants. It soaked the ground as it died at the necromancer's feet.

A sharp wind tore through the clearing and the drums stopped.

The people crouched—some crying, others silent—as a dark power seeped into the air like poisoned smoke.

I held my breath, as if that would protect me.

I knew better than anyone—there was nowhere to hide.

"It's the dark loa," one of the men hissed.

The bokor grinned like a madman, the white skull paint breaking into the wrinkles at the corners of his mouth, the black around his eyes making him look like a wicked demon. "The loa has blessed us." Feet bare, toes winding into the sandy soil, he stepped over the dead chicken and drew close to the struggling necromancer. "And now we have you as well," he said in a gravelly voice. "It took many moons to draw you to us. I was beginning to think we must slip that white gator into your bathtub. Call forth the loa in your living room."

Carpenter grimaced and tried to speak around the gag, his voice coming in angry, garbled bursts.

The bokor patted his cheek and turned to address the crowd. "It is the spirits of our ancestors who made us wait. They decided tonight was the night. They know the power of the blood moon." He stretched his arms out to the red-tinged full moon overhead.

The drums began to beat in a low, steady rhythm.

"Melona," the priest called.

A woman in white rushed to him, her head bowed. Hands shaking, she held out a plain, burlap sack to Pade. When he took it, she quickly bowed and backed away.

The corner of his mouth twitched in anticipation as he reached into the bag and drew out a heaping handful of dust. "We call upon our ancestors," he said, casting the dust into the fire. It sparked when it hit, sending up a billowing cloud of smoke. "The dead who live among us." He reached deep for another handful, scattering it over the fire. More smoke hissed from the flames. It was thick now, and I could smell the sweet, cloying scent.

The priest breathed in deep, his nostrils flaring, while I tried to do the opposite. I shielded my mouth and nose against my wrist. The smoke made my head feel light. I began to see shadows among the flames.

"He is ours," the priest said with relish, his eyes closed, his head shaking back and forth. He held a hand out. "Bring me the knife!"

Holy Hades.

The woman in white brought up a wicked-looking machete.

The smoke made the crowd go even crazier. They danced, their movements wild, the beat quickening. I stood. I had to get Carpenter out of there.

It was the last thought I had before Osse Pade grabbed the machete and sliced the blade across Carpenter's chest. He choked out a cry and bled freely. It ran in rivulets down his abdomen and onto the ground. I reached for a switch star as I caught the necromancer's wild-eyed stare. I didn't even know how he saw me in the tangled edges of the underbrush.

Carpenter shook his head no.

It was the only thing that could have halted me.

What the hell?

No telling how deep they'd cut him.

The priest now held the cup under the wound on Carpenter's chest, catching the streaming blood. If he drank it, I didn't know what I'd do.

I watched in horror as he poured it out over the dead chicken.

He clutched the cup, his entire body shaking. "We call to you, loa! We call to the mother of death!"

The feathers, soaked in blood, ruffled, and for a second I thought I saw the dead chicken twitch. But that was impossible and horrible and holy God—the thing started beating its wings against the ground. It had been dead, sliced open. Now it turned in a sick, struggling circle.

"The mother of death brings life!" the priest screamed as the drums pounded so hard I thought I was going to be sick, and the damned bird was actually alive and taking short, flying hops as if it needed to flee the noise and the press of the crowd.

But there was nowhere to go.

I had to get Carpenter out of there. They'd lured him, trapped him, and used his blood to bring a dead bird back to life. I knew better than to think it would stop there.

I drew a switch star and dashed straight past the startled worshippers toward the circle. Nobody stopped me. My legs felt hot as I jumped the fire, levitating to give me an added burst, praying I didn't overshoot as I landed directly in front of Carpenter. The smoke was thicker here, suffocating. The bokor reached for me. I elbowed him in the face, sending him sprawling into the dirt as I bent to slice open the bindings at the necromancer's feet. Pade grinned at me, blood running through his bottom teeth and down his chin.

Don't think about it.

My lungs burned as I unwound the rope from Carpenter's neck. The bokor knelt several feet away from me on the ground, bloody teeth clenched, arms raised, fingers winding towards me.

I began to see misty faces in the smoke.

Please let this be a hallucination.

Smoky hands reached for me. Hollow faces emerged from the mist. Their mouths moved as if to speak. Their voices crackled like the fire.

I freed Carpenter's hands, catching him as he stumbled forward.

"Run!" I ordered. I spun to avoid the disembodied figures in the mist. But they were behind me as well. I drew a switch star and threw it at them, hoping to break them apart. It cut straight through the smoke and disappeared.

The spirits weren't real. They couldn't be.

"The loa..." their broken voices called. "Embrace the loa..."

I felt the chicken flopping against my boot. I scooped it up, drew a switch star and used it like a knife to slice the bird's head off.

Screams erupted as the followers around me scattered and fainted. My own knees felt weak, but I forced myself to stay strong. I tossed the bird's body into the fire.

Osse Pade was nowhere to be seen, neither were his guards. Or Carpenter.

We had to get out of here.

"Carpenter?" I called, trying to see through the remains of the smoke. "Carpenter?!"

CHAPTER SEVEN

I dashed to where the clearing ended and out onto a large dock that clutched the swamp bank. Two guards and the priest had Carpenter in a black pontoon boat. I watched helplessly as it sped away.

My head felt thick from the smoke and my attention was so focused on them it took me an extra second to notice the guard staggering up behind me, his machete drawn.

He was off balance, too. He made a clumsy swing at me.

I shoved past him and ran full out toward the orange light of the bonfire. I had to get out of here or the witches would never know what had happened and we sure as heck wouldn't be able to help Carpenter.

Then again, I couldn't just leave him.

Osse Pade had lured him here. He was using the necromancer for his magic and I had a feeling this was only the beginning.

Think.

The fastest way out was straight through the mess. So that's the way I'd go. I skirted the moaning followers and the blazing fire, and sprinted straight through the underbrush and over the deserted land bridge.

I found Carpenter's boat where we'd first landed and jumped into it way too fast. My heart lurched as it rocked hard to the side. As long as I didn't capsize this frigging thing, I could do this. I could drive a boat.

At least in theory.

I started it up. *How hard could it be?* In truth, I didn't want to know.

A long handle thrust from the motor. I gripped it and steered out into the bayou, toward the smoke and fire and the chaos I'd just left. With any luck, I'd be able to discover where they'd taken Carpenter—without getting captured myself.

I focused my power and used it to open myself to the danger ahead. My demon-slayer senses craved anything that could drown me, burn me, chop me into fish bait, or leave me at the mercy of a crazy voodoo bokor. It was a pain-in-the-butt power, but one that would serve me well now.

I wasn't startled at all to discover they were all around me.

Fine. We'd do this the old-fashioned way. I skirted past the smaller island and rounded it toward the land bridge. There I saw a fleet of pontoon boats tied together. They stood mostly empty for now.

I slowed my engine, attempting to sneak past...

"There she is!" shouted a man on the shore.

I froze.

A red flare arced over the water and landed five feet in front of me, hissing as it sank into the bayou.

"Go, go, go!" I heard more of them yelling as they loaded into the boats. Engines flared to life.

I made a U-turn as fast as I could without tipping and opened up the motor, cursing myself that I didn't have any spells with me. I could really use a Mind Wiper, or six.

Demon-slayer weapons weren't made for boats.

The wind tore at my hair, the hard water slapping the hull and lurching the boat with bone-jarring impacts. But it didn't matter. I wasn't going fast enough. The roar of their boats grew louder. They were gaining on me.

The high-pitched whirr of an engine seared my ears as one of the pontoons drew up on my right. I drew a switch star and fired it into the hull. It sliced through it like paper and I realized with a start that this was the first time I'd ever fired while moving.

But the boat didn't slow down. In fact, it drew closer. And my switch star didn't boomerang back to me. It must be behind me. If it did arc back this way, I hoped to Hades it didn't slice through my motor.

The nose of the ship next to me dipped and I heard the whistle of my weapon directly behind my head. I ducked, grabbing it out of the air, the handles almost too hot to touch. I sheathed it as the boat next to me spun out.

With both hands, I banked hard left, nearly flipping over.

The out-of-control boat smashed into the pontoon behind it, tipping it and dumping my attackers into the murky swamp.

Waves rocked my boat. I clutched the motor handle, said a quick prayer, and steered toward a dark, narrow inlet. I had no idea where I was, where I was going. My demon-slayer instincts screamed to turn around and dive into the mess behind me.

But all the heroics in the world wouldn't help Carpenter when I was outnumbered and on the run. I had to be smart about this or neither of us would make it out of here.

I slowed, knowing it was dangerous, but I had to figure out where I was. I turned down another tight tributary. The canopy of trees above blocked out the moon, leaving me in almost complete darkness. That was fine. If I couldn't see, neither could they.

Water lapped against fallen logs and trees. Insects buzzed all around, their chorus broken by birdcalls and bullfrogs. It was the most crowded, loneliest place I'd ever been.

No telling how many miles of swampland they had out here, but it had to be a lot. Something splashed into the water next to the boat and I steered away from it, keeping as far as I could from the towering cypress trees, and wincing as water dripped onto my cheek and down my back.

The air felt hot even for night, the humidity stifling. I spotted the outline of something coming up on my left and nearly swooned when the familiar shape of the old shine shack came into view, the one Carpenter and I had passed on the way in. I used it as a beacon as the channel opened up.

Another island loomed ahead. I allowed myself hope as I picked up speed. This had to be it.

I wiped my forehead in relief as I saw the run-down dock we'd used earlier in the night. I tied up the boat and ignored my sea-weak legs as I ran for my bike.

It was still there. Thank heaven.

I rode it like an insane Red Skull back to the house, and I didn't stop there. I drove up the front walkway and parked it by the fountain before taking the porch steps two at a time.

Grandma had the front door open before I reached the top. "What's wrong?" she demanded, her heavy boots making the old boards creak as she stepped out and closed the door behind her.

My hair was tangled with sweat and clung to my cheeks and forehead. "I found the alligator and got rid of the black soul." I'd tell her how later. I dragged the hair off my face. "Only it was an ambush. Osse Pade has Carpenter."

A frown etched deep into the corners of her mouth. "Damn it. I knew this wouldn't be easy."

"They used Carpenter's blood to bring back a dead chicken."

She stared at me. "Fuck," she said under her breath. "I hate voodoo."

"I'm not a fan right now, either." At least of the dark stuff. "Pade's power is something else. I've never seen anything like it." I drew closer to her. "It wasn't just the chicken. He pulled spirits out of the fire. It may have been an illusion." But I wasn't going to take that chance. "I'm wondering if that's how he got those two black souls."

She winced. "This is bad, Lizzie."

"I got that. I stopped him tonight. They ran off before they could complete whatever ceremony he had planned."

"Doesn't mean he won't start right back up." She sighed. "I wish I could have seen what he had going with those spirits." She ran a hand over her face. "Those who practice voodoo—even the good and the light side—they claim our loved ones never really leave us when they die. They say our ancestors are near us, with us, on another plane that's a breath away from ours."

I didn't like where this was going. "Do you believe that?"

She gritted her jaw. "Nothing is impossible."

"We've got to rescue Carpenter." The sooner the better.

Grandma nodded. "Do you know where they took him?"

"Not exactly." I reached into my pocket for the purple flowers. "I found these where I last saw him."

"Drop them," she said.

I turned over my hand and let the flowers fall onto the porch.

Grandma crushed them under her boot. Tiny sparks shot out from under her heel. "Don't even touch his brand of voodoo," she warned.

I hated to break it to her, but, "It's going to be tough to avoid." In fact, there was nothing to do except focus on the problem at hand. "I'm not sure where they took Carpenter, but he did mention that the voodoo temple is on the edge of the bayou. If they were going to work magic on him, I'd have to think they'd start there. Pade also runs a business on Royal Street."

Grandma didn't even lift a brow. "Okay. Let's mount a rescue mission on the voodoo temple. If he's there."

"Sounds good," I said, without hesitation.

"I think I know how to find it. We'll get to work on the spells we need tonight, and we'll go in tomorrow after sunset."

"Can we speed this up?" Carpenter was in trouble.

"I'm not screwing up around voodoo," Grandma said, inviting no argument.

I got it. I really did. I hated to deal with the delay, but I also shuddered to think what would happen if they got the jump on us.

If the balls-to-the-wall, crazy leader of the Red Skulls needed a plan to go up against these ancestor spirits, I'd heed the warning.

And frankly, when it came to the safety of the Red Skulls versus the necromancer, I'd go with the witches every time. Carpenter was a survivor, just like me.

Grandma opened the door to the house and didn't seem nearly surprised enough when Ant Eater stood on the other side. "I've got everybody together outside in the backyard."

That was quick. "What time is it?"

"Just after one," she said. "We can still get a full night's work in." She glanced around the corner of the porch. "Creely and her crew are planting Light Eaters around the outside of the fence so none of the neighbors can see in."

Ironically the street in front of the house hadn't quieted down, either. New Orleans was crazy.

Ant Eater's gaze caught the sky, where the full, red moon hung low. "Good thing we have the blood moon. It'll amplify the power."

"As long as it doesn't make it go wonky," Grandma muttered. She turned to me. "Why don't you go rest up, Lizzie? You're going to need it."

I shook my head ruefully. They were dismissing me because, well, let's face it—my attempts to learn biker witch magic hadn't exactly been successful. My Mind Wiper spells put people to sleep. My Mexican Food Craving spell caused a run on Taco Bells in three counties.

And my one attempt at a Lose Your Keys spell made my neighbor's Kia Sorento disappear.

Still, I had to taunt the witches just a little bit. "You sure you don't want me to whip up any magic with you?" I asked it straight faced, trying my best to sound earnest.

Ant Eater held up her hands, as if she needed to protect herself. "No," she said quickly. Guilt settled over her features as she cleared her throat. "Conserve your power," she added. "We need you at your best."

I shook my head. "All right, then," I said, heading into the house. Frieda had a wooden crate of ingredients open in the foyer and was bent over it, passing back jars of heaven-knew-what to Edwina and Bug Eyed Betty. The glittering contents rattled the jars still in the crate.

I sidestepped two more witches carrying a barbeque pit. "Hey"—I turned—"where's Pirate?" He was usually at the center of everything.

Frieda glanced at me over her shoulder. "Your dog helped Creely make a nest for Flappy out back; then Pirate went to bed."

"While there are people awake?" Strange.

Frieda shrugged. "Top of the stairs, center room."

I shared a glance with Ant Eater.

"Grand-mère's room," she said, her voice thick.

It had been locked when we arrived. "I'm sorry," I said automatically. I had no idea how he'd gotten in there.

Ant Eater gave a slight shake of her head. If I hadn't been staring right at her, I would have missed it. "'S okay. Ask him if she's there."

I nodded. My dog had a certain affinity for ghosts, and he liked to make friends. "I'll check it out right now," I said, avoiding a biker witch with a blowtorch as I headed for the stairs. "You guys had better use those in the backyard," I added as I saw the blowtorch follow the barbeque pit out into the front.

"Good point," Ant Eater said, seeming to snap out of her haze. "Backyard brewing ceremony!" she shouted.

Several more witches rushed down the stairs, their boots pounding hard on the wood as they hurried to join.

I passed them going the other way, closing in on the pink-painted door that now stood ajar.

CHAPTER EIGHT

With a hollow breath, I pushed my way inside Grand-mère Chantal's room.

A faceted crystal chandelier cast uncertain light over the dusty room. Only three of the eight bulbs worked. The others remained dark, tangled in spiderwebs. I breathed in the stale air, the decay. A fireplace huddled to my left, its cold mouth gaping, the inside stained black with soot from long-dead fires. To my right stood an immense antique wardrobe.

At the very center of the room, a stunning gold bench strewn with pillows nestled against the foot of a rich, four-poster antique canopy bed. Dust marred the white canopy and pink silk bed coverings. My dog snuggled up near the carved mahogany headboard, on a stack of pillows, doing his very best impression of the princess and the pea.

"Lizzie!" He scrambled to his feet, scattering pillows.

I placed a hand on my hip. "Pirate Bartholomew Kallinikos, what are you doing here?" I didn't like this room. It was too cut off. Too...dead.

Except for the ten-pound troublemaker who had decided to camp out.

"I'm helping out a sweet lady," Pirate gushed. He dashed across the aged silk bed coverings and met me at the edge, shoving a wet nose into my palm. "Hmm...have you been at a barbeque?"

"Something like that," I said, scooping him up. I held him at eye level in front of me, his legs dangling. "This isn't the place for dogs."

Pirate liked to be around people, not cobwebs. Every canine instinct he had should have told him to stay out of this dark place.

"The door swung open," Pirate said, as if it were as simple as that. "Of course, I checked that out. Then—you're going to love this—I saw glittery magic lights. I just had to chase them."

"You don't *have* to chase anything," I said, knowing he'd never buy it. I folded him into my arms, holding him tight against my chest. "Ant Eater talked about the walls in this place bleeding. She didn't mention strange lights."

Pirate hit me with a cold nose to the arm. "No offense, but you're not very good at magic."

Wasn't that the truth? I scanned the room. Above us, the dangling crystals of the chandelier tinkled together. Cobwebs traced strange patterns on the faded silk wallpaper. "Do you see the lights now?"

Pirate wriggled against my strong grip. "They ran away, on account of my ferocity. But if we sit still, they might come back."

Not a chance. "We're leaving."

Pirate whipped his head to the right, then straight up, like he did while watching snowflakes. "Wait. There they are!" he exclaimed, profoundly impressed. "Ooh! They're bigger now that you're here." His hind legs dug into my chest as he snapped his jaws, trying to take a bite out of the air.

"Pirate," I scolded, wrestling to keep him in my arms. I still didn't see a thing.

"Ick," he recoiled. "Tastes like Healthy Lite dog chow."

"Come on," I said, heading for the hall.

"No." My dog burst out of my arms and landed hard on the floor. I reached for him, but he sidestepped me. In a move he'd perfected for the vet's office, he zigzag dashed across the room and belly-crawled under a large dresser draped in a dirty lace runner.

"Pirate," I warned, stalking up to his hiding place. "Come out from under there right now." Perfume bottles crowded the surface, their rich scents reduced to crust under glass.

"She's worried about us," my dog pleaded, his voice muffled under the dresser. I saw a paw peeking out.

"Who?" I asked, making a grab for him. *Oof.* Just missed. My back crinked and I stood for a second, my eye catching a framed black-and-white photograph of Chantal Cerese Le Voux amid the scattered perfume bottles. The photograph showed a smiling, younger Chantal, wearing a classic party dress and posing with a dapper-looking man at her side. I took it and slid it under the dresser. "Is this lady talking to you?"

The doorway to the bathroom lay just beyond the dresser. I gave a small shudder. That's where she'd died.

"She's real nice," Pirate said, his tail thumping against a dresser leg. "She says don't talk to the spirit in the tower, and I say, 'Of course not. I'll stay right here with you.'" His tail thumped against the carpet. "I think she's just lonely."

No, she was smart. We were going to heed that warning and get the heck out of Dodge.

I followed the sound of the tail and found Pirate's entire rear end sticking out from the far end of the dresser. Ha. I grabbed hold of his back haunches and dragged him out from under the dresser. "Time to go."

"She's my friend," he said, trying to dig back under.

"You don't have to make friends with everybody." Pirate couldn't save the world. None of us could.

"I'm a dog," he said, struggling, "it's my job."

When I'd gotten him almost, sort of under control, I saw that I stood in front of the open doorway. Watery light spilled into the white-tiled bathroom and over an old-fashioned claw-foot tub against the wall. A cold draft filtered from the room, prickling over the bare skin of my arms.

My dog sighed. "You're so pretty."

"Thanks," I said, shivering against the sudden chill.

He wriggled in my grip. "Not *you*," Pirate said, looking into the bathroom. "The lady in the tub."

I tightened my grip and stared.

But I saw nothing—only the shadowy outline of the empty tub.

Pirate tilted his head at the icy presence. "Sorry. I don't do baths unless forced. They make me stink."

My dog had an affinity for ghosts. He sometimes saw them when I didn't.

"Mrs. Le Voux?" I asked, wondering if I was indeed out of line for talking to the woman while she was in her bath. "Thanks for the warning." We'd crash in one of the biker witches' beds, or in the kitchen for all I cared.

Pirate's tail whacked against my arm. "She says we can stay right here in her room." He craned his neck to me. "He's waiting for you outside."

Okay, that creeped me out on about ten different levels.

I backed away from the door. The light from the bathroom had begun playing tricks on my eyes. I blinked against the halos clouding my vision. The fog in my brain thickened as I forced myself away.

Pirate felt heavy in my arms. "Okay, now we should run," Pirate said, scrabbling against me. "Lizzie?" His voice swam in my head. I kept walking. Backward. I wasn't going to leave my back exposed to the spirit.

Keep moving.

"You don't look so hot." Pirate's nose nudged my arm. "I think we'd better stay."

Sure. In a haunted room. Maybe I should just take a bubble bath while I was at it.

My shoulder hit the wooden bedpost. The bed shook. My shoulder throbbed, but not as much as it should have. Alarm registered in the back of my brain.

"Pirate—" I clutched at the bedpost and struggled to sit on the edge of the mattress. It would only be for a minute. I just needed to clear my head.

It took all my focus to shift Pirate to my left side in case I needed my right hand for my weapons.

He wiggled out of my grip and onto the bed. "Lizzie, are you all right?"

"Yes," I said, hearing my voice slur.

It was worse than I thought.

We had to get out of here. I tried to shove myself to my feet, but it was like I'd hit a sharp, icy wall. I fell backward onto the bed, my head throbbing, and the mattress soft beneath me.

Pirate curled up, warm at my side.

"Cold," I managed to say.

His nose hovered over my cheek, his warm breath puffing against my skin. "Don't worry," he said, his hushed tone betraying his concern. "I'm the best watchdog in Georgia."

But we were in Louisiana.

"I'll protect you," Pirate assured me.

That was the last thing I heard before everything went dark.

†††

I woke to the sensation of warmth on my skin, along with a slow, prickling unease. I had to get out of there. I reached for my dog, but he was no longer at my side.

"Pirate?" I whispered as I sat.

The room glowed with an unearthly light. My dog wasn't on the bed or on the floor. He'd most likely gotten himself into trouble.

As I scanned the room again, I could sense a presence above. Watching me. I wrapped my arms around my chest and darted my eyes to the ceiling. But I saw only the crush of milky white fabric where the canopy stretched overhead.

Misty light filtered from the bathroom, along with the distinct sound of water trickling over tile.

I was not about to go in there and see if the tub was overflowing.

Instead, I looked away and saw another door near the corner of the bedroom. The same light filtered from its edges and from where it hung slightly open, big enough for a curious dog.

I sat up straighter as the door creaked and opened wider. I sure hoped he wasn't up there. I rubbed my arms. "Pirate?" I called as loudly as I dared.

He was getting no doggie treats for a year. No Bow-Wow Brownies, no Schnicker-Poodles. And he could forget about any Paw-Lickin' chicken bites.

With a clear head and a healthy dose of oh-my-God, I cautiously approached the door in the wall. It hadn't been there before, or at least it had been hidden from me. I ran my fingers over the place where it joined with the patterned wallpaper, amazed how seamlessly it blended. I never would have picked it out if it had been closed tight.

It felt warm, alive.

I pushed it all the way open and found a small, narrow staircase leading upward. Rays of light shone from the top, like the heavens reaching down. All right, then. I rested a hand on my switch star belt. I had a sinking feeling that I knew exactly where this led. And I didn't like it one bit.

It grew warmer every step I took, the stairs creaking under my feet.

The door at the top stood open. I braced myself and walked straight through it, right into the séance room in the tower.

My face flushed with the heat. Charms dangled from the ceiling. I hadn't noticed them before. They turned in slow circles, tinkling together. I stood in stunned silence. I'd never wanted to come back here.

I stared down at the Ouija board on the center table. The planchette rattled against the board. I watched with dread as the game piece spun slowly and stopped, pointing directly at me.

"Hello, Elizabeth," a male voice oozed.

My heart sped up. A trickle of sweat ran down my back. "I'm not talking to you," I murmured to myself, not to him. *Never* to him.

The small room grew even warmer. "I knew you'd come back."

Quite a trick, considering I'd never wanted to set foot in this place again.

Whatever this was, *whoever*, seemed to exist in the air itself. I tried for shallow breaths, pulling only as much into my lungs as I dared.

This had to be a dream, I realized, as the steaming air washed over me. I clenched my nails into my palm, trying to wake myself.

Wet breath tickled my ear. "You like my power."

"No," I answered. I couldn't help it. His presence was suffocating. "I'm just here for my dog."

He laughed at that. "Refreshing. But you and I both know he's not here."

He appeared to be telling the truth. I didn't see any trace of Pirate. My dog had been smart enough to stay out of here, away from this…presence. I could feel it watching me even before I'd come to this room.

It had been premature to tell myself we were okay after we'd locked up the tower, that the witches had secured the house. We should have suspected a hidden entrance or at least searched for one. Whatever this thing was would always have a back door.

I tried to retreat to the stairs, but my body wouldn't move. It was as if I'd lost all control. I could do nothing but stand and stare at the tinkling chimes, and breathe in— breathe out—as the air grew hotter and thicker all around me. I began to pant. Was I under his power?

"Calm yourself," he tsked. "I'm trying very hard to be friendly. You can at least do the same."

I opened my mouth, not trusting my ability to speak. "I—" I gasped. It felt like someone had stuffed a pillow over my mouth. "I need you to leave me alone."

He let out a low chuckle. "Just the opposite. I was willing to help you tonight. But when I made myself known, you locked the door and left. How very foolish."

My entire body flushed with heat. "I didn't need helping."

"You of all people should know that's not true," he drawled, slipping into a slight Southern twang.

My mind swam and I struggled to keep from passing out. "You can't do anything. You can't even leave the house." Whatever this thing was, it had limits. The presence had evaporated as soon as I'd walked out the door.

"The witches can brew all the spells they want under the blood moon, but you saw real blood tonight, didn't you, Lizzie?"

"This conversation is over." I fought hard to move, to escape.

"You are a treat," he said, far too pleased, "so I'll warn you. All blood is not the same. Do you understand?"

"Yes," I said, pushing until my eyes watered, until my body burned. I'd seen what they did with Carpenter. I understood the power in play.

"There's more," his voice rumbled in my ear. "All bones are not the same, either."

"What does that mean?" I demanded. Were they going to skin Carpenter alive? Cut him apart?

"Go," he ordered.

I lurched out of bed, gasping for air, shocked as I sat in the gray light of dawn, panting.

It took me a moment to realize where I was. I shook, drenched with sweat, and felt the weight of Pirate curled next to me, asleep. I stroked his back, my clammy hand catching on his fur. I needed to touch him to make sure he was actually there, to know that I wasn't trapped in the tower room, with…whatever that was. "It wasn't real," I murmured.

All blood is not the same.

I'd seen it with my own eyes. I'd watched it play out in the smoke and the fire of the voodoo rite.

"Please, don't let it be real."

All bones are not the same, either.

That one scared the hell out of me.

Chapter Nine

Enough.

I pushed out of the bed, my movement rousing the dog. At last.

"Hey, whoa." Pirate rolled to his feet as if he hadn't just been curled up, lights out a few seconds ago. "You're awake," he said, perking up, his back legs going airborne as he shook off. "I kept you close the whole time."

"Thanks, buddy," I said, at a loss for what to do now that I'd made my way to my feet.

There was nothing to push up against, nothing to fight. The room felt eerily empty now. Quiet.

I needed to see if that door in the wall was actually there.

The light from the chandelier flickered as I ran my hands over the age-stained wallpaper. Heaven knew what I'd do if I found it.

My fingers danced over Greek vases filled with baby roses, laid out in an intricate diamond pattern. Up close, the design made me dizzy. Or maybe it was the quivering light. It made it even harder to locate any irregularities. Each of the roses was made of a velvety material that felt soft under my touch, while the rest of the paper was smooth silk. Of course, any sort of opening wouldn't be obvious, nothing that merely anyone could find.

Unless it didn't exist at all on this plane. Maybe it was just a dream.

This place—this mission—had a way of making me lose track of what was real and what wasn't.

My gut clenched when my fingers snagged on a narrow crack where two sections of the paper met. I followed it with my fingertips until the gap fused into more roses, more faded silk paper.

Damn.

I followed the same gap, or at least it seemed like one. It was on the line of the paper, so it could be that. I wedged a fingernail under the silk and tried to pull it back, but the frigging wall covering was stuck on tight. After so many years, it was part of the wall.

That rose pattern was burning itself into my brain, giving me a headache. I scrubbed a hand over my eyes. If I'd walked through that door, if I'd seen the spirit, it had knocked me out on purpose and kept me here until dawn.

I dropped my hand. Heck, maybe I was just exhausted after battling alligators, releasing a black soul, witnessing a voodoo rite, and then fleeing for my life. It had been a busy night, even for me.

I bent to study the wood base paneling near the floor. It was carved with Roman-style floral designs and much easier on the eyes than those nightmare roses. The baseboard would also be the perfect place to hide a lever or a handle. I focused on every nook and cranny. If it was here, someone had hidden it very well. I sat back on my heels.

If the only way to open it were located on the inside...then I would try not to let that bother me too much. I stood, exhausted even after several solid hours of sleep.

I just didn't know...

It was probably just as well I didn't find a door. I wasn't about to head up there without six witches and an arsenal of protection spells. And even then it was iffy.

Pirate's tags jingled as he jumped off the bed. "You done staring at the wall?" He ambled over to the large dresser and gave it a sniff. "The real fun is in the dresser. I'll bet there's lots of socks to play with."

"Not now." I tried to think. The darkness I'd felt in this room before...I'd bet it was coming from the spirit in the tower. It was the only way to explain the energy shift since I'd woken up. It was as if he'd gotten what he'd wanted from me, and now it was my move.

Pirate jumped up on the bed. "How about you try to take a pillow and I'll hold onto the same pillow and you can drag me around by my teeth?"

"I'm thinking," I told him.

"It's a very easy game," he said.

"Right." I turned my back on him and tried to get everything straight in my head.

The spirit had set out to frighten me, to get a rise. It had worked on about ten different levels. But there might also be something behind his warning. For better or worse, he'd known what had happened at the voodoo ceremony tonight. As to whether or not he could predict what would happen next...I wasn't about to take anyone or any*thing* for granted, not with so much at stake.

Still, I had to remember, it had been a dream. Our latest encounter may have existed only in my head, not upstairs, not in the tower room. When you got down to it, "it might not have been real."

Only deep down, I knew that it was.

✝✝✝

I headed downstairs, with Pirate on my heels. We heard the clomp of boots in the kitchen and found Ant Eater tracking dirt across the linoleum floor. I glanced at the unused doormat and then back to her in a sweaty tank top and her hair pushed back off her forehead with a red bandana. She thunked two huge spell jars onto the center butcher block and stepped back to admire them. "Who-ee," she chortled. "These babies will burn the tits off a boar."

"Oh, yeah?" I challenged. "How about the feathers off an old voodoo bokor?"

She smirked as she considered the question. "That too."

The sun cast orange light through the windows behind her. I could hear the voices of the witches, and the hiss of at least one blowtorch outside in the backyard. They'd been at it the entire night.

"Thanks again, for this and for everything." I honestly didn't know what I'd do without the Red Skulls.

She cast me a wily look. "Just remember that next time a batch of Cherry Bomb spells escape."

Yuck. They'd fled right during dinnertime. My taco tasted like someone dumped cherry pie filling inside. "Why do you even need cherry spells?"

"I'd be out of my damned mind to take my arthritis medicine without cherry flavor."

"Perish the thought." The witches were so rough and tough and then we'd get…cherry flavor. I should probably tease her about it, but I had other things on my mind. "Listen," I said, trying to shift the focus to more pressing matters. It wasn't the best time to break the news, but we had to face this. "There might be a back way into the tower we sealed yesterday." At her curious glance, I added, "Saw it in a dream. A secret entrance off your grandma's room."

"Damn it all." She leaned both hands on the butcher block. "By the tub in the bathroom?"

"On the other side. Near the bed."

She dropped her head. "Fuck." She pushed off the counter. "I'll ward off the entire suite. It'll trap, well, everything in there," she said, planting her hands on her hips. "Should have done it yesterday."

"Hey," I said, placing a hand on her arm, trying to stop her as she started to pace. "You did good. Bringing us here, keeping us safe. We appreciate it, you know."

She narrowed her eyes.

I kept going. "I'm glad to have you on my side."

Things certainly weren't as simple as I thought they'd be.

The witches didn't have to support me like this, especially now. It wasn't their duty or their job to follow me down here. They'd done it because they cared about me, and I wasn't about to take that for granted or pretend it was easy for any of us.

Ant Eater gave a sharp nod. Her gaze traveled over her grand-mère's sturdy kitchen. "She was a good person." Her eyes darted to me and then away again. "I'm not sure what she got caught up in. Or what happened at…the end. But I'll always remember her the way she was."

"It's all you can do," I said simply.

We both jumped as Grandma and Frieda banged in the door, each carrying a cookie tray loaded with what appeared to be rubber crazy balls. The blue, gelatinous insides churned with a life of their own.

"I've never seen those before," I said. They rolled against each other, sparking when they touched.

Ant Eater huffed behind me. "Go ahead. Pick one up."

Nice try. "This isn't my first rodeo," I told her.

"You don't need to be playing with these," Grandma said. "Not until you get your dog out of our breakfast." She pointed to Pirate crouching in front of the open cabinet door, Cheerios scattered at his feet. When he saw we were onto him, he began to eat faster, shoving his entire head into the box on the floor.

"Pirate," I scolded. No wonder he'd been so quiet. "We don't know how long those have been in there." I took the box, and when he began sniffing and gobbling frantically for stray Os, I picked him up.

"The food's fresh," Grandma said, reaching past me for a box of breakfast bars on the middle shelf. "We made a run last night." She didn't even try to avoid the mess. Her boots ground stray bits of cereal into the floor as she dug a peanut butter breakfast bar out of the cabinet and tossed a second one to Ant Eater.

I winced at the crumbs that were surely getting…everywhere. "I hope you brewed up a housecleaning spell last night."

"That's about the last thing on my list," she said, unwrapping her breakfast. "I think we've got everything we need for tonight. Some of it's still dripping. Creely and her team built some drying racks, and then the Sneak spells need to hide in the shadows in order to set up right." She shared a nod with Ant Eater, as if that last part were obvious.

"We just need to figure out where they're keeping Carpenter," I said.

Grandma began rooting around in her pocket. "That's why we conjured up this little sucker." She drew out a Ziploc bag with what appeared to be a regular housefly inside. It didn't glitter. It didn't glow. It rammed up against the plastic, as if it could force its way out.

"I'm surprised it's in one piece," I told her. She could have easily crushed it.

She watched it whack its head over and over against the plastic. "Spell bugs are tough." She gave it a little shake. "You told me Osse Pade has a business on Royal. I made a few inquiries. He's going to be out that way at about ten this morning. You go, you plant this bug on him, and we'll be able to track him."

I liked how she thought. "I could mix in some uncomfortable questions about Carpenter, just for fun."

"Yeah." She nodded, her gaze traveling over me. "You look like hell."

Like I needed the reminder. "Bad dream," I said, holding out my hand for the spell bag. "Give it here. I can handle this."

The knife rack rattled behind me, as if begging to differ.

"I'll go with you," Ant Eater said. "I don't trust that guy."

"I don't, either," I told her. "But it'll be less suspicious if it's just me. He already knows I'm after him. You guys are my ace in the hole." I wasn't going to take a chance on blowing that, on letting him know what was coming. "He can't suspect I have any kind of special help. I'll go and be back within an hour."

Grandma chewed at her thumbnail. "She's right. It's better for Lizzie to do this on her own," she said to her second in command. "You need sleep."

"How does it work?" I asked, eyeing the bug. I had to make sure I got the spell on Osse Pade instead of me or anyone else.

"The bug wants to land on something. Anything," Grandma said. "Launch it at the bokor when he's not looking. As soon as it connects with him, it'll disappear and go into stealth mode. Osse Pade won't even know he's carrying it."

"Nice trick," I said, tucking the spell into a side pouch in my utility belt.

"It's new," Ant Eater said, with a hint of pride. Lucky for me the Red Skulls never stopped innovating.

"You all mind if I take a look at the spells you brought and borrow one or two for my trip over to Osse Pade's?" I couldn't be too careful.

Grandma grinned. "Take what you want. We packed plenty."

They did indeed.

Maybe the witches could give me some insight on my other problem. "The spirit in the tower talked to me in a dream last night," I told them. "He spoke about blood and bones. It may have something to do with their plans for Carpenter."

"Don't," Ant Eater said quickly. It surprised me. She was usually the one blazing forward, damn the consequences.

"It can't hurt," I said, somewhat defensively. "If he let something slip, we'd be that much ahead. He said *all bones aren't the same*."

Grandma shared a glance with Ant Eater and shook her head. "You should know better than to listen to strange spirits."

"Oh, come on—" I started. "This one's making sense."

Ant Eater gave me a squirrely look. "Resist the temptation."

If only it were that easy.

††

I took an extra-long shower in a bathroom off one of the guest rooms and thought about how I wanted to approach Osse Pade. I had to look nonthreatening. I had to blend if I wanted to get close enough to plant the bug on him. I also knew better than to try to hide what I was. It wouldn't work, and the bokor would see it as weakness.

A straightforward plan was best. I'd let him know in no uncertain terms that his actions had attracted the attention of a demon slayer and that he'd have to deal with it.

I changed into a simple black leather dress and matching boots. I tucked the enchanted emerald necklace down between my breasts and styled my hair into a simple ponytail at the nape of my neck. Then I buckled on my demon-slayer utility belt with the five switch stars holstered, ready to throw, hoping the voodoo bokor had enough magic to see it. And enough arrogance to ignore a simple housefly.

I left my bike in the backyard of the house, preferring to walk over to Royal. Burgundy Street was pretty this time of the morning. Lush plants dripped from wrought-iron balconies and I caught the distinct beat of jazz music filtering out of a house or business nearby. As I drew closer to the touristy section of the French Quarter, I passed shopkeepers, out early, hosing off the sidewalks from the night before.

The sound of the trumpets and the beat of the drums grew louder as I approached St. Phillip Street. Then I reached the intersection and saw it. Well, I heard it first. The tinkle of a piano and then to my surprise, the entire instrument along with the man at the keys, sitting high up on the back of a metal trailer dragged by a red pickup truck. A seven-piece brass band marched along with it. The men wore suits and swayed to the music. An old-fashioned horse and buggy hearse trailed behind them, with an honest to God skeleton in the front seat, driving. Well, he wasn't driving. My world hadn't gone that strange yet. Eight pallbearers marched, four on each side, leading the empty carriage. They came from the direction of the large cemetery north of Rampart.

A family trailed behind, holding on to each other. The men sported white suits, with colorful ties that matched the brims on their white hats. The women's colorful dresses caught in the morning breeze. Clutching their hands, in the middle of this human chain, was Osse Pade. I recognized him immediately, even without the eerie white skull paint on his chest and face. I'd know those high cheekbones anywhere, that expressive face, those wicked black eyes. He wore his white top hat tilted rakishly to the side with yellow feathers thrusting out of the brim.

He didn't see me in the crowd.

It was on.

I followed him, joining the parade of mourners twirling umbrellas and singing "When The Saints Go Marching In." It seemed death was a celebration.

Just what kind of business did this man own?

I kept sight of him up with the family as the procession continued down St. Phillip and then made a left onto Bourbon Street. These people were not trying to hide. We picked up a bunch of tourists on Bourbon. Them in their colorful mourning wear. Me in my simple black.

"Nothing to see here," I murmured. Just a demon slayer carrying a spell bug, joining with voodoo church members to celebrate a jazz funeral.

We made a last minute left on Barracks Street and hit Royal, trailing past Voodoo Works, the shop where I'd met up with Carpenter. The owner, Aimee, watched us through her glass front window. She caught my eye and nodded. I kept walking.

We stopped about a half-block down, in front of a funeral parlor. Only this was nothing like the subdued, tasteful mortuaries I'd seen growing up in Georgia. The building facade was painted purple for starters. Columns flanked the front entrance, decorated in orange, gold, pink, and black swirling designs. Even the sidewalk displayed chalked skeletons at a party. It shouldn't have surprised me that Osse Pade would own a funeral parlor, even one like this.

I smiled for the first time since I'd joined their party. Maybe I'd come out of this with something to celebrate as well.

Chapter Ten

I moved quickly through the crowd outside the funeral parlor. Already, church members had begun to call out their goodbyes and hug one another as they filtered to the cars parked along the street. I'd have to move fast if I wanted to catch the bokor by surprise.

He stood near the front doors. A simpering older woman clutched both of his hands in hers and kissed his knuckles, thanking him over and over again. Now was my chance. I reached for the bug.

Osse Pade turned as if he could sense the danger. His eyes widened when he saw me.

Damn.

I was too far away to launch the spell, at least without him seeing me. I shoved it back into my utility belt.

Osse Pade watched me as if I were about to bite. "Go, Esmerelda," he said, dismissing the woman with an absent wave.

At least I'd caught him off guard. He hadn't anticipated any trouble or he'd have made sure his goon squad stood nearby. I noticed the way he scanned the sidewalk and street, and found no sign of them.

"Your watchdogs are out by the hearse," I said, pleased to find my boots made me almost as tall as him. "Talking to pretty ladies," I added. Couldn't resist.

He gave a shallow smile. "I'm talking to one as well." His voice was hard, his Cajun accent strong. He took my hand and leaned down as if to kiss it. He licked it instead.

I felt the slide of his wet tongue over my skin for a split second before I yanked it away. Jerk. In the same motion, I reached up and smacked the top hat off his head. "Do that again and you're going to lose more than your hat."

Nonplussed, he bent to retrieve it. As he rose, he made a show of donning the hat, running his fingers along the brim. "You taste better than I expected," he said low, his eyes glittering with interest. "There's something wonderfully...dark about you."

"You need to work on your fortune-telling." It was exactly the opposite. I considered it my job to stamp out as much evil as I could in this world. And this clown had earned a spot at the top of my list. I cocked my head. "I'll tell you one thing: I am a woman to fear."

He smirked. "It's not you, girl." He licked his lips and prepared to lean closer, before stopping himself. Wise move. "It's *him*." He teased the air with his fingers, as if he could see it. "He soaks up the space around you. A master presence."

He could be lying through his teeth to intimidate me. I'd be overjoyed if that were the case. But there was no mistaking his keen attraction and, worse, his effort to tamp down his excitement.

This was not going according to plan. He was paying far too much attention to my every move. I needed him distracted.

I eased toward the building and felt the pressure of the wards. They pushed at me like two polar opposites of a magnet. No big surprise he'd have it well protected. I wasn't getting in there without an invite.

Pade focused his attention on the space near my neck. The priest was besotted. If he were a cat, he'd be purring. "Tell me his name."

"It doesn't matter," I said quickly. I hadn't asked it. I'd ditched that presence in the tower room.

Oh, Elizabeth. A chill slammed through me as the spirit spoke. *As if you could leave me behind.*

Sweet Jesus. It was in my head now? I locked my shoulders, refusing to give an inch. Hopefully then Pade wouldn't see me shaking. He seemed to grow more enthralled by the second. "I'm here to talk to *you*," I said to the bokor.

He drew back. "Then you misplayed your hand."

Two guards approached from the sidewalk. I recognized one from the swamp. Each held on to a weapon inside his jacket.

I scrambled hard to think.

"What if my dark presence wants to commune with you?" I asked. I was grasping at straws and inviting the worst.

This could be a big mistake.

The bokor paused, sizing me up. "You do know he's there," he said slowly, as if he'd caught me in a lie.

"How would I not?" I asked, terrified at the thought.

That's right, how could you not? the spirit echoed in my head. He had gotten to me somehow.

"Let's do this alone. Inside," I added, eyeing the guards.

I could see that I'd tempted him. The bokor tilted his head and removed his hat. "Very well," he said, opening the brightly painted front door for me. As if I'd just walk into a trap. I had a few tricks up my sleeve as well. And the good sense to wait.

I felt the zing of his wards, like needlepoints on my skin as I crossed over the threshold, but I'd been granted permission. I was in.

And the guards were still several yards away. Their mistake.

The bug required a quiet, secret release, but not this next spell. I spun quickly toward the doorway and reached into the back of my utility belt, withdrawing a Ziploc baggie with a twirling black and white striped spell inside. I tore it open. I'd had a good feeling when I borrowed it this morning, even composed a little enchantment to make it mine.

"It won't work here," Pade said, as if it were a matter of pride.

"Thanks for the warning," I said, releasing the live spell in the doorway. It zipped upward like a trapped bottle rocket. I raised my hands quickly and began the enchantment before the goon squad realized what was happening. "Guard all points." The spell zinged to the bottom of the doorway and up, then back down, and up. It was downright beautiful. "Let no one through." I tried to hide a giddy surge as sparkling, nearly transparent magical bars appeared in its wake. "Except for me." And, yes, I'd planned this part for my new friend. "Trap the bokor, too."

"Cute," Osse Pade smirked, but his smugness evaporated when he flung a hand out at the bars, only to have it flattened by an invisible barrier. The look on his face almost made me feel sorry for him. But not quite. "Impossible," he seethed.

"Your guards are also asleep," I said, pointing out the two slumping goons by the hearse. Lucky for me, the rest left for the party.

Pade turned to me, barely containing his rage. "You planned this."

"Of course I did." Silly man. I loved that he underestimated me. And that the magic had worked for me. Spells sometimes went haywire when I tried to use them, but this had been worth the risk. "Let's have some alone time."

"I don't suppose I have a choice." He turned on his heel and stalked through the lobby.

I slipped the bug out of its Ziploc bag and prepared to strike from behind. Then I stopped cold.

Ornate designs in white chalk swirled over the parquet floor of the lobby, reaching toward the edges. I recognized hearts and crosses inside large patterned swirls and geometric shapes. This place was spelled. Not surprising, given the circumstances. Still, I had no clue what these symbols meant or what they could do to a person.

Osse Pade strode confidently over the marks, shooting me a glance over his shoulder as he did. Great. An unspoken dare.

I clenched my hand. The bug struggled in my grasp, its wings stinging my palm. I may have won this last round, but I'd be a fool to get too cocky.

"I'll stick to the scenic route," I said, keeping to the narrow section of clear floor near the walls. It took longer, given that the room was long and narrow, but I wasn't one for taking unnecessary chances.

I walked tall, past yellow walls streaked with thickly painted images of death. A skeleton in a top hat smoked a cigar while a serpent wound through an empty eye socket. Another appeared to have been skinned alive. It smiled and wore a necklace of bloody fingers.

Classy.

The bokor smirked as he waited for me near an altar at the back. The surface was crowded with bottles of rum, lit candles, playing cards, stuffed animals, candied nuts, even cash tucked into nooks and crannies. "Your master spirit should make you brave," he challenged.

Just the opposite. He scared the hell out of me.

"Who is he?" the bokor pressed.

I stopped in front of him. "Wouldn't you like to know?"

"You'll tell me eventually," he said, keeping an eye on me as we walked through a wide archway.

The man was on perpetual high alert. I bided my time as we passed into an open brick-walled courtyard. The morning sun shone down over rows of rickety white folding chairs. They lined up in front of a low stone altar caked with colorful wax. I noted, with a prickle of alarm, that the stone floor sloped gently downward toward a metal drain below the stone slab. Behind it, a raised dais awaited the next coffin.

The open structure of the building made me willing to bet they still had Carpenter out at the swamp. It would be hard to hide a prisoner here. The only other inside space was behind a simple wooden door on the left side. The bokor headed that way.

He slipped a key into the lock, and we entered a dark, narrow room. The cloying scent of incense competed with the musky odor of old death.

He lit a large candle and I soon saw why. The thick red taper sat upon a real human skull. Shreds of leathery skin still clung to the empty nose socket, stained red with dripping wax.

He lit more candles, some in holders, some on low bookcases lining the walls. The shelves held more skulls, as well as framed pictures of individual people, and personal effects like a harmonica, a beat-up flask, and a feathered fan. I also saw leg bones, fingers, all human from what I could tell.

I caught his glance.

"Nice bones," I said.

The candlelight flickered over his sharp features. "My ancestors are close to me."

He said it like a warning. I didn't bite.

In fact, I didn't move at all as he bent and opened a rickety drawer in the old apothecary chest behind him.

Now was my chance. I closed in quick, releasing the bug. It circled toward me for a moment, confused. I swatted it back, praying it wouldn't land on me.

Osse Pade let out a cry and turned, faster than I'd ever seen him move. He had his hand up, fingers pinched, ready to strike.

I met him halfway, making a grab for whatever he was ready to toss at me. The bug buzzed around our heads, as if it couldn't decide whom it wanted to infect.

Just before I could close my hand over the bokor's
pinched fingers, he let loose a dash of gray powder. I
flinched as if stung and refused to inhale as it fluttered over
me.

For a second, we both froze.

Then I shoved him back. He hardly noticed. His eyes
were wild, his breath coming in pants. "Now," his voice
boomed. His every word was pronounced. "Tell me what
you are."

The bug landed on the side of his neck and melted into
his skin as if it had never existed.

I wiped the dust from my nose and cheeks. "I'm a demon
slayer." I'd gotten him and he'd gotten me. I gave myself a
quick once-over. So far, I wasn't burning or bleeding.
Nothing was falling off. Yet. "You do that again, you'll get
a switch star through the head."

He drew his brows together. "There is no such thing as a
demon slayer."

"I'm about two seconds away from giving you a
demonstration," I snapped. I'd wanted to be more cagey
about this, but not if I was under attack. "Now tell me,
where'd you put Carpenter?"

He stared at me, his breathing heavy and his manner
unsettled. "Don't play games with me, little girl."

"I wouldn't dream of it," I said, advancing on him. He'd
attacked me. We weren't pretending anymore. "I saw you
take the necromancer."

He reached into his pocket and pulled out a small leather
bag, similar to the one he'd used in the swamp. His lips
curved into a menacing smile. "In the fog, it's hard to tell
what you truly see."

I grabbed for it. He avoided my grasp, and damned if I
didn't see the bag anymore.

"Cut the bullshit." Yes, the fog had been as unsettling as
my dream last night. Maybe I was having trouble telling
what was real and what wasn't, but the voodoo bokor had
slipped up. He'd brought up the fog, and in doing so, he

might as well have admitted that I'd walked into his ceremony in the swamp—that I'd seen things I shouldn't. I took hold of his arm and pulled him close enough that my breath whispered against his cheek. I'd rather not think about where I'd suddenly gotten that kind of physical strength. "I know about you, Osse. I was there."

A rivulet of sweat trickled down the side of his face. "You invaded my ceremony. You walked through the spirits of the dead," he added, as if he could hardly believe it himself. He pointed a long finger at me. "Yet you are not a necromancer."

"No," I agreed, gritting my teeth as I held him tighter. "You tied the necromancer to a post in the ground."

The bokor sneered. "He deserved it."

He shoved away, and I let him go. "Push me and you're going to find out exactly what a switch star is."

I wouldn't kill him. Not if he wasn't attacking. But I'd sure as Hades redecorate his office.

He held his wrist where I'd gripped him, and again, I marveled at my sudden strength. "It's not wise to threaten me when I hold your friend's life in my hands."

He had me there, and it made me angry as hell. I fought the urge to circle him, to surround him. "Did you lure Carpenter there?" I demanded. "Was the black soul in the alligator a way of trapping him? You bled him, you sicko."

His dark gaze held mine. "Sometimes, one must suffer for the greater good."

The bones of the dead rattled on the shelves next to me.

"You used his blood to resurrect a chicken. Then you drove off with him in a boat," I barked. "I tried to be reasonable. I tried to come here and have a simple conversation with you, but the people I'm with, they want to destroy you." The witches had learned to fight evil without asking questions. Maybe I was a bleeding heart, but I'd been willing to talk. To live and let live. "I'm just trying to get the necromancer back."

His face hardened. "No. Not when he hurts the people I love." He took one deliberate step toward me, then another. "I will fight. I will die for her."

"Who?" I demanded, watching him shut down. He wasn't going to tell me. It didn't matter anyway. "Let my friend go. Stop tangling with black souls, and we'll leave you alone."

"Get out," he ordered. "Leave my church. Leave me in peace."

He was a fine one to talk about peace. "I'll go," I told him. "But I'm on you like a tick until you release Carpenter." And even then, I couldn't make any promises. Not if he tangled with another dark soul.

He stalked toward me, hovered right over me, his forehead slicked with sweat. "Then be like your friend," he challenged. "Test me. Just don't expect to win."

CHAPTER ELEVEN

Grandma opened the door while I was still halfway up the porch. A red bandana held her hair back and charcoal smudged her right cheek. "You bug him?"

"Yeah," I said. "He didn't make it easy."

She gave me a quick once-over. "Don't tell me you got hexed."

"Have a little faith," I said automatically. Then again, he had sprinkled that dust on me. From the way he'd acted, I gathered it was a truth powder. I held my hands out to the side as I approached her. "Do I look like I got hit with something bad?"

She rolled her eyes. "People don't go around looking cursed."

I gave a snort. "You've obviously never seen me hungover."

She rested a hand on her hip, giving me a great view of the new butterfly tattoo on her wrist. "Well, the good news is you'd never make it through my wards if you were a shambling zombie."

"That's why you're in charge," I said, moving past her and into the foyer.

She let me go. "You find out anything at the funeral parlor?"

I let out a long sigh. "Osse Pade is deluded. And powerful."

Grandma groaned. "My favorite kind of guy."

I sprawled onto the settee just inside the door. "He seems to think whatever he's up to is a good thing, but he won't admit where he's keeping Carpenter." I leaned my head back. "I don't think he has him in the city." It would be too much of a risk. "Carpenter still has to be in the swamp somewhere."

I'd tell her later about the spirit that seemed to be hanging around me. I didn't want to give it attention, even in my thoughts. That seemed to be what it wanted, and so far, it hadn't hurt anything. I rubbed my itchy eyes. Now that I'd reached the relative safety of the house, I realized how tired I was. "I need to lie down for a few minutes."

"Before you fall asleep where you're sitting... Here." She tossed me a round ball the size of a quarter.

I caught it in one hand. It was glittery and blue. Slippery, too. I worked hard to keep hold of it. "What's this?"

She closed the door. "Sneak spell for tonight. Stick it in your bra. Let it warm up to you. It'll work better that way."

"Of course." I shouldn't be surprised. This was custom biker witch magic. I nestled the charmed sphere down past my bustier top and into my cleavage. "Just so long as it doesn't try anything," I added, eyeing her as the spell wiggled a bit. I jammed it in there tighter.

Grandma grinned. "The way you're built, I'm more worried about the damn thing suffocating."

I had to laugh. "Hey, at least I know where I got the gift."

Grandma didn't know when to quit smiling. "Speaking of things nestling in your cleavage—"

"Are we really going there?"

"Your husband called," she continued, not missing a beat. "He'll be here tomorrow."

Fantastic. I was more relieved than I wanted to admit. "We could really use him." Dimitri was strong and powerful, plus he had a great instinct for getting us out of trouble.

"I didn't tell him you were out chasing down dark voodoo."

He'd assume. Nothing much got past him. "Hopefully, we'll have Carpenter back by the time he gets here." I could wish, anyway.

Grandma nodded. "In the meantime, I've got something to show you."

I pried myself off the couch and she ushered me into the living room to the right. About two dozen camouflage backpacks lined up along the pink-papered walls.

"More spells?" I asked.

"All packed and set to go. Didn't seem right for me to crash until we had everything ready. And until we had you back. I told the rest of the coven to head upstairs." We continued toward the dining room in the back. "We need 'em sharp for tonight."

We passed through the arched doorway and I drew up short. "You didn't…"

Grandma looked like the cat who ate the canary. "Creely said you'd be speechless."

"I said I hoped." The engineering witch chuckled as she leaned over the big table. "I knew better than to think it would happen."

I scanned the room, amazed. The witches had transformed the place into a war room. Detailed topographical maps hung from the walls. I saw weather reports, the star and moon positions. A huge city map was spread across the dining table, held flat by spell jars. "How did you get all of this together so fast?"

Sure, Creely had built a trebuchet in an afternoon. She'd taken mere hours to reconfigure magical griffin armor into a defense shield for Dimitri's ancestral villa. But that was hands-on. This was…research.

Creely shrugged, the Kool-Aid-red tips of her hair brushing her shoulders. "It's my job."

"I'm also shocked you guys are planning," I said. I was being honest, not trying to insult them.

Grandma shared a glance with Creely. "She acts like we can't learn anything new."

The engineering witch huffed. "Good thing we can or we'd still be letting Sneak spells mingle with Chocolate Cookie Craving spells. We'll never get all of those back under control."

Creely motioned me over to her position in front of the map. "Now look here. Whatever you said to your voodoo friend must have worked. About twenty minutes ago, he made a beeline out of the funeral parlor and out toward the swamps. See?" She laid a thin silver film over the map and I watched a glowing red line appear. "This is his trail. The guy's a regular speed demon." It went from the French Quarter, down the highway Carpenter and I had taken, out toward the swamps, and it was still moving.

Damn. "You're better than Q in the James Bond novels."

"Of course," she said, "I'm a woman."

"Look here," Grandma said. "He's stopping."

He was. The red bug paused at a lush green spot on the map, surrounded by water.

Grandma paused in front of a map on the wall. "The topographical overlay shows a series of small buildings in the area."

Probably a moonshine shack as well. "That looks close to where we were last night," I said. The small peninsula lay deep in the swamp, yet close enough to skirt a highway.

"You see this road here," Creely said, her finger following a winding tan line through the lush green peninsula. "This is a back way in, so we don't have to try to fit everyone into boats."

"We don't even have boats," I murmured, warming up to this back-road idea.

"We could get boats if we needed 'em," the engineering witch muttered.

"I don't doubt it for a second," I told her. I studied the winding road out of the swamp. "There's a low bridge before you get there. Except for that, the road leads directly to the highway."

"Ideal for a quick escape." Grandma nodded. "We'll have to be stealthy."

The Sneak spell wriggled in my bra, as if it knew. "Thanks for this." I wasn't sure Creely truly understood how much we needed her. "As usual, it's more than I expected."

She kept her head down, her eyes focused on the map, but I could tell she was pleased. "Your grandma wants to go in after sundown."

"Good plan," I said, turning to Grandma.

She rubbed at one of her eyes. "You should think about taking a nap. You look like hell."

That made two of us.

Although after last night, the mere thought of sleep made me distinctly uncomfortable.

"I'll just hang out in the lodge room," I told them. I didn't want another chat with my buddy upstairs. Besides, the snarling, stuffed wild game would keep me awake.

"That center room's still open," Creely offered, "although your dog is bunking down with Sidecar Bob."

"I'm fine," I said, letting them climb the stairs. I chose a leather couch framed by curtains that appeared as if they'd been clawed apart at the bottom. I could handle the spirit situation and the bokor. I just had to hold out for a little while longer.

†††

"She's alive!" I felt a wet tongue on my ear and hot doggie breath on my cheek. I opened my eyes to see an excited Pirate right in my face. "I told you she wasn't possessed," he said, happy in a way only dogs could be, as if that were my greatest accomplishment today.

"I haven't been possessed since..." I trailed off. Well, it had only been a couple of months ago. I reached out to rub the scruff between his ears. "I'm sorry about that, by the way."

"It's okay," Pirate said, his eyes shining with sincerity. "I love you."

I groaned to a sitting position, scooping up Pirate along the way. I held him to my chest. "The world would be a better place if we all thought the way you do."

He licked my hand.

The couch rattled. Heck, the whole house probably did, as witches thundered down the stairs like an invading army. It's a wonder I'd slept through any of it.

Frieda approached me, looking more like a swamp creature than her usual, zebra-print, fabulous self.

"Does this ghillie suit make my butt look big?" she asked, clearly joking as she chomped on her gum. The brown and green full-body camouflage was layered with loose strips of burlap strung with leaves and twigs. She fiddled with a stick near her shoulder. "We'll pick up some swamp doodads too, once we get there."

"I think I'll stick to my demon-slaying outfit." My powers and my weapons depended on my ability to maneuver.

"Suit yourself," Ant Eater said, wearing a suit and holding a stick of face paint. "Come on, Frieda. Let's make you beautiful."

The blonde witch tilted her head up. "Or at least invisible." She had a stocking cap stuffed in her belt. I'd never seen the witches try to blend before.

"You look like Lady SEAL Team Six," I told them.

Ant Eater began slicking Frieda's face with the paint. "If that's what it takes to get in and out."

The front door hung open. Several witches had pulled their bikes out front. I saw them strapping duffel bags onto the backs.

Creely plopped down next to me with a map in her hand. She'd folded it to where only the swamp part showed. "We'll park our rides behind this curve in the highway here," she said, pointing to the winding stretch of road. "We'll find a place where the trees are thick. After that, we hoof it toward our first likely location. When we get a hundred yards out, we release the first Sneak spells."

"Got it," I told her. "I'll take the lead." I had the best weapons.

Osse Pade might be looking for me anyway. But he sure as heck wasn't expecting the Red Skulls.

†††

We closed in on our target shortly after sunset. At a signal from Creely, the witches pulled their bikes off the highway onto a spot that looked like any other maze of trees along the secluded bayou roadway.

In less than a minute, the bikes were hidden under tan tarps made to look like leaf-strewn ground.

The biker witches had brought *tarps*. I tried not to let that blow my mind too much.

Instead, I focused on the sizzle of dark magic in the air. My demon-slayer senses urged me forward into the swamp. I stuck to the shadows on the side of the narrow dirt road and motioned the witches to follow.

The emerald at my neck warmed as I strained to see into the pitch darkness in front of me. The moon was high, but it did little to help me navigate the swampy ground tangled with tree roots and littered with holes. I slowed, hoping the biker witches were behind me. I didn't hear them. I turned and realized with a jolt that they were nowhere to be seen.

Sweet heaven. "Grandma?" I hissed.

Had something gotten hold of them already? Or perhaps I'd been overeager and lost them. Fear rippled up my spine. I felt...alone.

"Grandma," I said, louder this time, my heart beating hard. They couldn't just disappear on me.

A hand closed over my left arm and quick as lightning, I drew a switch star with my right.

"Whoa!" Grandma said, low and harsh. "Take it easy." I still didn't see her. "I'm right here. Just got a Sneak spell in my bra."

I whooshed out a breath as I sheathed my switch star. "How'd you turn on the camouflage?" I didn't do anything to the spell in my bra.

She shook her head, her face a shadow. "You don't have to."

"Were you invisible back there?" I hadn't seen her.

"No, just hard to notice. They work best in the dark."

No kidding.

"Now relax," she said, letting go of me. "We're all here."

"Right," I said, moving forward again. According to Creely's map, we'd walk about a fourth of a mile and make a hard left at a narrow dirt path. I didn't see any guards. Not yet. But I had a feeling there would be plenty coming up.

They were holding Carpenter nearby. I felt it in the heaviness of the air, in the wisps of dark magic that lingered just beyond reach. I could almost hear him calling out to me. I could almost feel his pain along with the ties that bound him.

I increased my pace, letting go of my need to plan each step I took, letting my demon-slayer senses take over as I navigated the uneven ground. I didn't slow, not even when my emerald necklace began to hum.

The chain thickened and turned to soft, warm metal. It slithered down my chest and wound around my left arm like a snake.

At least it wasn't my throwing hand.

I'd refused to admit it out loud earlier, but my drop-in on Osse Pade's horror house had left me more confused than enlightened.

Demons I was used to. They were power hungry, pure evil, and quite transparent in their desire to slice my soul into a snowflake chain before snuffing me out completely.

Osse Pade had a fascination with death, black souls, and something else he refused to name. And he held sway over the kind of spirits that could haunt me into the next generation.

Worse, we didn't know his end game—or what he was capable of.

We came up on a path to the left that led to a low bridge over the water. Torches burned on either side, as if they expected us.

It looked like a trap.

No wonder Carpenter hadn't come this way last night. I ducked to the side of the path and raised a hand to tell the witches to hold up.

Grandma eased up next to me. "Nice," she muttered. With an underhand toss, she launched a round, black Sneak spell at the bridge. It bounced over the wood boards and sent up a vibrant magical shockwave. I felt it more than I saw it.

She gave a hand signal and Ant Eater advanced, with Frieda covering her.

When Ant Eater reached the edge of the bridge, she lobbed another Sneak spell into the center before she proceeded forward. At the middle, she threw one to the end. It seemed they covered about ten feet in any direction.

"It's not good to just wear them?" I whispered to Grandma.

"Usually it is. With so many of us going over that bridge, this is added insurance."

Okay. Got it.

She held up two fingers and that seemed to be our cue.

Grandma nudged me. "Come on."

A chorus of frogs croaked as we hurried across. No telling where they came from all the sudden, but I was thankful the noise covered the creaking of the wood under our feet.

When we joined Ant Eater and Frieda on the other side, I realized the witches were the source of the noise. Ant Eater let out two short croaks, and within seconds, a chorus sounded from all around us.

"Everybody's in position," she told Grandma.

I tried to see the witches through the trees. It was impossible. I could barely see the ones right next to me. "How'd they all make it to the other side?"

I could hear rather than see Creely's grin. "Bridge. Some also used deep-swamp maneuvers." She shoved something into my hand, and when it nearly slipped out, I realized it was a Sneak spell. "An extra in case you need it. Wait. One more."

I gave her a quick nod and shoved them both into my utility belt.

We pressed forward several yards until we saw the light of more torches. Men's voices filtered out over the bayou. Whoever they were, they didn't bother to hide.

"You do not need to hurt him. Leave that to the bokor," one chastised.

"Ah, but he is so easy to tease."

They had to be talking about Carpenter.

Grandma patted me on the back as I took the lead, drawing one of the Sneak spells from my belt. The creature in the back of my utility belt snarled, as if it were inconveniencing him. Useless beast.

"Who is that?" The massive head guard from the other night stepped from behind a tree, blocking my way. I slammed the Sneak spell onto the ground in front of him. It exploded like a firecracker.

"What the hey?" I protested.

"She's here!" he shouted.

The burly guard drew a potion from his pocket.

"Run!" Grandma ordered.

My botched spell began darting around, out of control.

Grandma fired off something of her own as I dashed past. I heard the whoosh of magic behind me as the witches joined in.

I didn't know what had gone wrong, except that I sucked at magic. I hadn't added anything to the spell. I hadn't had time.

Up ahead a round hut stood surrounded by burning torches. Drums sounded in the distance. I didn't know what was in that hut, but every demon-slayer instinct I had screamed at me to launch myself at the danger inside.

Decision made. I drew a switch star and shoved open the simple reed door, only then seeing the symbols scrawled over the surface in thick, rusty blood.

I stopped short.

A single lantern lit the dingy space. Carpenter hunkered under it, shirtless and barefoot, wearing the same pants he'd had on last night. They were stained with blood and he had an open wound on his side. But it was the look of horror on his face that halted me.

He held out a hand, as if to block me. "Don't come any farther," he ordered.

Fine. "The guards are distracted. Let's go."

He swallowed hard, not moving an inch, bracing himself as if he needed all his strength to remain upright. "I can't."

Of course he could. I took a few more steps inside. He wasn't even tied up. "This is ridiculous," I said, ready to drag him out if I had to. "The witches can't hold them off forever—"

He shot up. "Don't cross the barrier!"

I stopped at the edge of a white painted line on the ground. It surrounded Carpenter. He stood in the center of the circle.

His breath came in pants. "It's hexed."

Frick. They had him bound in a way I hadn't expected.

No matter. "I get that the bokor is powerful, but you've got to come with me. Just try it." We had to push through this. "Your blood brought back a dead chicken, I don't even want to think about what your bones could do."

"My bones?" The necromancer shook his head. "I know the danger." The fear was written on his face. "I can't move out of this circle. I tested it earlier by luring one of my guards in."

"What happened?"

"His blood boiled and he died."

Wow. "Okay." My mind raced for a solution. "We'll figure this out."

His eyes glittered with anger, like a tiger trapped in a cage. "I can't do a damned thing...except be glad as hell I got you into this," he muttered under his breath.

That made two of us. He wouldn't survive here long on his own. "If I'm going to help you, you've got to be straight with me: What do they want with your blood?"

He shook his head slowly. "They're trying to resurrect something, I don't know what." His shoulders drew tight, his lips thin.

We had to think. "All blood is not the same," I said, repeating the words of the spirit in the tower. "And all bones are not the same, either."

Surprise flashed across Carpenter's features. "You might be onto something."

"If I am, then you'd better tell me." We didn't have time to screw up.

He nodded sharply. "Go back to Aimee at the white voodoo shop. Ask her to take you to the grave of the Three Sisters."

"Lizzie." Frieda pressed the door open behind me, the smoke of the fight pouring in around her.

The battle had moved closer. The witches fought guerilla-style, hiding behind the huts, tossing Paralyzing spells at the advancing, machete-wielding guards. They exploded in showers of silver sparkles, toppling the guards mid-stride, mid-thrust, mid-attack. But it seemed like every time one went down, two more took his place.

Frieda and Ant Eater had been flanking the entrance to the hut, protecting me.

Ant Eater leaned her head in. "We're running out of ammo. We gotta get out of here."

"One second," I told her. I turned back to Carpenter. We wouldn't be able to take him with us. "I'm sorry."

He steeled himself. "This isn't on you."

I knew that, but I hated feeling powerless to get him out. "I'll ask Aimee about magical circles. Also, what are we looking for in that grave?"

"Aimee will know," he assured me. "Please be fast."

I nodded, turned, and as I left, I heard him add, "I just hope it's still there."

Chapter Twelve

I nearly tripped over a renegade Paralyzing spell as I dashed out of the hut. "Let's go!" I hollered.

A guard came at me from the side, the same one who'd trapped me in the tree. The purple stripe down his nose glistened with sweat as he reached for me. Ant Eater hurled a spell jar over my right shoulder and it slammed into his chin, taking him down in a rain of silver sparkles.

"Bat out of Hells!" Grandma announced over the din of the battle.

The ground shook with a series of explosions. Frieda grabbed my arm and dropped a coal black jar down onto the ground in front of us. The impact rattled my teeth.

"Run," she said, still holding onto me. Together we bolted faster than I could have ever imagined. It felt like flying.

The huts whooshed past us, the trees. I barely saw Creely and Edwina covering our escape as we dashed across the narrow bridge. My joints clattered from the impact of my feet on the hard boards.

Frieda suddenly released me and I stumbled forward several feet. We were back at the clearing off the highway and I realized with a start that most of the bikes were already gone.

Good.

Motors groaned as witches surged up the hill and onto the road. Frieda tossed the tarp off her bike and drew a potato launcher off the back.

She hefted it over one shoulder like a soldier with a bazooka. "Duck," she ordered as she leveled her weapon and fired a shot that splotched in a wet mess near the tree line where we'd come from. The steamy vapor singed hot on my cheeks.

It sent up a cloud of green mist that completely enveloped everything behind it. "Grandma!"

She burst out of the mist with Creely, Edwina, and Ant Eater on her heels. "Go, go, go!" she hollered.

I hitched a leg over my bike and punched the throttle.

The green smoke thinned. Beyond it, I saw staggering bodies approaching across the swampland. It had to be the guards, fighting the effects of the Paralyzing spell.

Ant Eater and Grandma fired up their bikes behind me, along with Creely and Edwina. "Everybody's out!" Ant Eater announced before gunning it toward the road.

Everybody but Carpenter.

†††

I hit the open road, guilt searing my chest. It about killed me to leave Carpenter alone in that place. Sure, he put on a brave face. I'd have done the same. But there was no getting around the fact that he was a prisoner in an enchanted circle, kept so they could use his blood.

Engines roared all around me, but I couldn't actually see any of the coven. It was the oddest feeling. I'd be glad to get rid of these Sneak spells.

I pressed on along the remote road, trying not to dwell on Carpenter. If they were willing to bleed him, I shuddered to think what else they might do. They had him alone and powerless. I only hoped that what we'd find in the cemetery would change that.

As we neared the city, the witches tossed their Sneak spells. I kept mine. I'd need it soon.

The coven regrouped along the highway and rode in formation, with Grandma at the lead and Ant Eater bringing up the rear. I stuck close to Grandma, not because I was in charge of this bunch, but because I needed to talk with her.

I got my opportunity after we exited the highway and took Tulane down to Rampart Street and turned into the French Quarter. It was slow going, what with the tourist traffic and the partiers out on the streets.

Surprisingly enough, no one paused to take a second look at a bunch of Harley riders wearing camouflage suits dangling with sticks and fake birds.

At least Frieda had stashed away the potato shooter.

Perhaps we couldn't compete with the bars offering colorful drinks and beads and live shows. Or maybe those Sneak spells took time to wear off all the way.

Police on horses had blocked off several of the side streets, including Bourbon Street, which was just as well. It would take us twenty minutes to make it down that way. I used the opportunity to motion for Grandma to cut her engine.

I still had to holler over the rest of the Harley noise. "I'm going to find a way to get down to Royal Street and visit that voodoo shop again. The good one," I added over a cheer from the revelers as somebody earned a string full of beads. "Carpenter thinks his friend can help us."

Grandma drew a gloved hand over her chin. "Okay. I think I've got enough to take her down if we need to."

It wouldn't be necessary. "Carpenter trusts her." She should be okay. "I want to talk to her without an army at my back." I didn't know any woman in her right mind who would take kindly to a squadron of biker witches, their spells locked and loaded, showing up at her door after dark.

Besides, I could defend myself.

Grandma pressed her lips together and huffed. "Then you and I will do it together." Before I could respond, she cut me off. "Voodoo is dangerous, Lizzie."

No kidding. "I got that loud and clear."

Grandma gave a sharp nod. "We'll drop the coven off and then head back."

"Right," I said, agreeing to the new plan. I just hadn't expected the surprise that awaited us when we returned to the house.

Chapter Thirteen

Dimitri Kallinikos, my husband, best friend and real-life dream man, straddled his bike on the street just outside our safe house. I let out a small, very uncool scream and was ready to ride straight up to him and dismount, when Grandma gave him the signal to follow the group of us around back. So I had to wait while he rode next to me and grinned.

Tease.

I didn't have the patience tonight. Not after what we'd been through. I was hopped up and nearly bursting with adrenaline.

We pulled into the backyard. The witches lined up in rows. I parked along the outside, next to Dimitri. He was off his bike and kissing me before my engine had fully shut down. I wrapped my hands over his strong shoulders and breathed in his warm male scent mixed with motor oil and leather.

After the darkness, the pain, the struggle this trip had brought, I finally had a ray of light and I wasn't about to take it for granted. I eased off my bike and wound my body closer to his, very glad to feel firsthand how happy he was to see me.

"Get a room," Frieda said, brushing past us, her potato gun hoisted over her shoulder.

"It would be our pleasure," Dimitri murmured against my lips.

It would also be quite a feat considering our current living quarters. We had biker witches sleeping upstairs and down, some of them five to a room. And there was no way I was going anywhere near the bedroom at the top of the stairs.

All righty then...

I took Dimitri's hand. "This way," I said, urging him toward a small garden in the far corner of the backyard, away from the house. Wild roses overgrew the arched entryway and vines had overtaken the trellises.

"I didn't even see you until you screamed." He chuckled behind me.

Yeah, well, good thing I still had my Sneak spell—although I doubt the biker witches ever thought of using it for something like this.

Dimitri trailed a hand down my spine as we ducked past a leafy tangle of morning glories grown over a lilac bush full to bursting with blooms. The tangle of wild plants created a maze of sorts, a memorial to faded glory.

He kissed me and drew me deeper into the garden, past a marble fountain with a wrought-iron viewing bench. A stone wall at the back dripped with Spanish moss. I felt my back hit the wall.

He cupped my cheek. "Remember the last time we did it outside?"

I closed my eyes at the exquisite feel of him running his fingers through my hair. "I believe I do," I answered, coy, as I found the spot behind his ear that he loved. "I came," I whispered, nibbling at his lobe, enjoying his inhaled breath. "Spectacularly."

Our entire family had also caught us, including my mother. I'd longed for him then because we hadn't been able to get a second to ourselves during our wedding week. Now I craved him for an entirely different reason. After days on edge, I needed to know that there was something good in the world, something right.

"You're going to make me lose my mind," he said, his words labored. His breath came harsh against my neck. "You know that."

"It's part of my charm," I said, sliding my hand along the front of his jeans. He hissed, pushing into me so I could feel just how hard he was for me.

He was always so primed and ready. I pulled his jeans open and reached inside, eager to drop to my knees and show him exactly how much I appreciated that.

He lifted me into his arms instead, pulling me into a deep kiss. I surrendered to it as he carried me farther into the garden. I wrapped my legs around his hips and ground into him, making him moan as he deposited me on the ornate bench behind the fountain.

"Are you wet for me?" he asked, teasing his fingers along my pussy in a way that made me feel them even through my leather pants and panties.

"Soaked," I said, feeling myself grow even hotter for him.

He grinned. "Show me."

I flipped the button on my pants, and together, we drew them off my body, with my panties still attached. I lay back on the bench. I was done teasing. I spread my legs and let him see for himself.

I think I shocked him. In fact, I know I did. His face dropped and he stared with pure lust.

"Now what are you going to do about it?" I asked.

He crushed me to him, kissing me hard and urgent. God, I'd needed this.

He trailed wet kisses down my neck and across the top of my chest. "Fuck. You drive me insane. You do it on purpose, don't you?"

The corner of my mouth tugged up. "Yes." I gripped the back of his head when he drew down my bodice, my fingers tangled in his thick, short-clipped hair. I jerked when he ran a hot tongue over my aching nipple. "Careful," I gasped. "I've got a Sneak spell between my boobs."

He jerked his head up. "What'd you say?" His gaze was lust-drenched, glassy. His calloused fingers rubbed at my nipples, sending a jolt of fire straight between my legs. He gave a slight shake of his head. "Forget it," he mused, his voice thick with desire as he bent his head down to my breasts. "I don't care."

And as he kissed and sucked and licked my breasts, I found I didn't care, either.

I gasped as I felt the tip of him against my entrance. It felt so good. "Get on with it," I murmured as he wet his head in my juices, making me push against him, trying to get more of him inside me.

His breath burned hot against my cheek. "What? You think I'm a sure thing?"

Jerk. "I know you are." I thrust up against him, taking more of him inside me, driving both of us crazy. It was one of the things I loved about him. We didn't play games, not when it counted. He was on my side. Always. I could depend on him no matter what.

"God, yes," he said, thrusting deeply. "You're my world." He reared back and shoved forward again. "My everything." He kissed me deeply. "I love you."

"I love you, too," I murmured against his neck. "With everything I have."

And I was desperate for him, for the way he made me feel. For knowing that I could pour out my love and my lust, my fear and my pain, my anger and my hurt and that he would take it all. With Dimitri, I wasn't alone anymore.

I held him tight and felt my eyes grow hot with tears as I squeezed them shut and let my body buck and scream and come apart with the pleasure of it.

I felt him stiffen as he gripped me tighter and his thrusts came quicker. He lost some of that control, his breath coming in pants as he pushed into me with growing desperation. He moved with a razor-edged need. He gasped wetly against my cheek and with three more hard thrusts, he came inside me.

He went limp and heavy on me, and I found breathing overrated as I ran my hands over his broad back and shoulders, relishing the fact that he was back where he belonged.

"So I take it you missed me," he said, pulling away slightly, grinning like some kind of superstud. Then again, I supposed he had every right.

"I did," I informed him. "Next time, I'm just going to kidnap you."

He gave a wolfish smile. "Now that's got to be more interesting than clan meetings." He shook his head slightly. "Although not by much. Those guys are crazy."

"You'll have to tell me all about it," I started, "but right now…" I shifted. Now that the lust had worn off a bit, I noticed my butt had fallen asleep on the hard metal bench and I wasn't sure how he'd gotten my boots off. My toes were starting to get cold, even with my ankles wrapped round his back.

"Ah, the perils of outdoor reunions," he said as we untangled ourselves. He drew me back into his arms and I snuggled against him on the bench, with my legs tucked under me.

"Let's go inside," he suggested.

"Not yet. But we should get dressed," I said, reaching for my pants. I hated that we didn't have time to linger. "I need your help."

He nodded, all business. It amazed me how quickly he could go from sex-on-a-stick to badass griffin. As he stood and grabbed for his jeans, I knew there was no one else I'd rather have with me that night.

"Our favorite necromancer…" I began.

"Carpenter," Dimitri grunted, grabbing his riding boot.

"Right," I said, buttoning my pants. "They captured him when we went to take the black soul out of that alligator."

Dimitri planted a foot on the bench to tie his boot. "It never goes according to plan, does it?"

"The alligator was bait, for Carpenter. They're using his blood, Dimitri. The voodoo bokor took it and brought a dead chicken back to life."

Dimitri straightened.

"That's not all," I said, glad to have his full attention. "This voodoo bokor, Osse Pade, I think he wants to use the necromancer's blood for something worse. We can't free Carpenter. He's in some kind of voodoo cage and he wants me to go to the grave of the Three Sisters. Osse Pade is obsessed with his ancestors and I think it has something to do with that."

He pulled his shirt on, his movements stiff. "You don't know what you'll find?"

I double-checked the Sneak spell lodged deep between my breasts. "It can't be good." Dimitri followed my every movement when it came to my cleavage. Men. "In voodoo, there's a light path and a dark," just like there was with witchcraft. "I met a light practitioner a few days ago. She knows Carpenter. He said she can take us to the grave of Osse Pade's ancestors."

Dimitri gave a quick nod. "Seems smart."

"There's also a presence in the house back there. It's been trying to get to know me. Yesterday, I could actually hear it in my head."

Dimitri's eyes widened. "Then we're not going back inside."

"That won't help," I told him. "I don't need to be in the house to hear it. I think I just need to stop thinking about it. I don't want to give it power."

He cursed under his breath. "I should have gotten here sooner."

"There's nothing you could have done." He couldn't fix everything.

Both of us were fully dressed. If anyone found us now, they'd never believe we were out of control in the bushes just a few minutes ago.

He drew me close and brushed a kiss over my forehead. "We'll figure this out."

"I know," I said, taking his hand and leading him out of the peaceful garden.

Rows and rows of bikes lined the yard, all facing toward the exit, ready for a quick escape.

"Be careful," Grandma warned from the porch.

"We will," I called to her. We didn't know Aimee well. She was Carpenter's ally, not ours. But you couldn't have darkness without the light. If Aimee were that light, I'd be a fool to pass this up.

"I won't let anything happen to her," Dimitri said as we turned our bikes toward the road.

Grandma frowned, as if she had a bad feeling. If I was going to be honest about it, so did I. But we couldn't back down now. I strapped on my helmet and gave a sharp nod to Dimitri. Whatever we'd find, we'd face it together. With that thought in mind, we fired up our bikes and rode out into the night.

Chapter Fourteen

Two blocks later, we ran into the nighttime party crowd. It had grown thicker since we'd come back from the swamp. I motioned to Dimitri and we cut a sharp left, bypassing the worst of it as we rode toward Royal Street.

The section of the Quarter near Voodoo Works offered fewer bars and nightclubs than the party streets. It held more antique shops and other specialty stores that closed at eight or nine o'clock. Still, when we reached our destination, plenty of people strolled up and down Royal. And I noticed several entering Osse Pade's funeral parlor down the way. I resisted the urge to drive down there and check it out. Not yet.

Instead, we parked in front of Voodoo Works. The purple and yellow neon sign glowed, but the placard in the crowded front window read *Closed. Have a blessed evening.*

Too late for that.

"This is Carpenter's friend?" Dimitri asked, eyeing the skeleton posed in the front shop window. Today, it wore a colorful turban and held out handfuls of gris-gris bags.

"They've been sharing information," I said, rapping on the door. Although I didn't think he'd ever planned to trust her with his life. I tried to see into the shop. Perhaps Aimee was still working.

A single security light in the far back corner cast an uneven glow over colorful display tables stacked with candles, dolls, and soaps. Near the back, wind chimes hung from the tin ceiling. Only I could swear I saw one of them move.

I knocked again, and a large, dark object fluttered, letting out a muffled curse as it banged against the chimes, setting off a chorus of high-pitched tinkles and bells.

"Aimee?" Maybe she had a guard...bat.

One with a potty mouth.

"It's Lizzie. I need to see you." I should have gotten her cell number.

I gave a quick glance behind me and found Dimitri scanning the shadowy street. He gave a slight nod. He had us covered from that direction.

The shop had quieted down again. Obviously, my rapping at the door had done no good except to wake a pet of some sort, one that was too lazy to sound the alarm.

It flapped its wings and retreated into a back room.

Maybe she was in there.

"We're going 'round back," I called, remembering the alley I'd passed when I'd come here the first time. "She might be doing inventory in the storeroom," I said to Dimitri.

He motioned for me to show the way. "Let's hope."

The narrow alleyway smelled of old beer and garbage. The back doors didn't have street numbers or any signage that I could see, but I'd bet anything Aimee's was the purple one with the flaming heart and the evil eye painted across it. I dodged the large flower pot filled with geraniums and braced myself before I knocked.

Please be there.

If something could be done tonight to help Carpenter... I didn't want to wait until morning.

"It's Lizzie," I said, rapping at the door.

No response.

"The demon slayer," I added, knowing Aimee was one of the few in this city who would believe me.

No response.

"I brought my husband, Dimitri," I said, in case she looked out and grew worried about the huge man at my back. "Carpenter's in trouble."

Something metal clanged to the ground. Then I heard her voice. "One moment."

The door cracked and Aimee peered out. Her curly dark hair tickled her flushed cheeks and hung wild about her bare shoulders.

Oh my. "We're sorry to interrupt," I said quickly.

Her face shone with perspiration. "I was in the middle of a ritual," she said, clearing her throat. "Let me get my robe."

Dimitri averted his eyes. Now I'd seen everything.

"Naked rituals?" he asked. A wicked grin tickled his lips and he gave me a nudge. "Maybe you should stop trying to learn spells and start up a voodoo practice."

"I'll get right on that," I said dryly, as if he didn't see me naked enough.

Aimee opened the door as she shrugged into an orange silk number. She tied the belt as she motioned us inside. "What happened?"

We stepped into a claustrophobic back room with a candlelit altar to the right, and shelves of glass jars, herb-filled baskets and who knew what lining the left wall and every other spare inch of wall space. The air hung heavy with magic.

That wasn't even the weird part. I stared at a full-sized hot tub, shaking as it hummed, and taking up almost every bit of walking space.

"How relaxing," Dimitri mused.

"Never mind that," she said, waving off the concern.

Right.

I tried not to stare at the thing, but oh-my-god she'd filled it with muddy water and twigs and bits of floating grass. With a jolt I wondered—despite what the necromancer said—if it was wise to team up with a woman like this.

"Listen," I said, hoping we were correct to trust her. "Things have gone wrong. Osse Pade captured Carpenter and is keeping him trapped in a magic circle. He said it was too dangerous to break him out. He told us to come to you for help."

"What did it look like?" she asked.

"A white circle on the ground, with lots of squiggly lines coming off it in all directions."

She handed me a piece of parchment and a pen. "Draw it."

I sketched a hasty picture, trying to remember each shape as best I could. At first glance, the markings had appeared random, but I knew better. There had to be some kind of meaning behind them.

Aimee drew a sharp breath even before I'd finished adding the spikes around the edges of the circle.

"A twisted veve," she said, as if the very words were evil.

"Can you break him out of it?"

She visibly paled. "No, I cannot. This is strong dark voodoo."

I'd had a feeling. "Okay, we'll go to plan B. Carpenter told me to take you to the grave of the Three Sisters."

She made a quick sign of the cross. "Aye, Madre, what's there?"

"He said you'd know."

Her forehead furrowed. "I don't know what he's talking about."

"Maybe you'll know it if you see it," Dimitri suggested.

She cast a worried glance to her altar. "Perhaps. But my husband isn't home. He'd have my head for going there."

"I know the feeling," Dimitri mused.

Feelings aside, we didn't have time to wait. "I don't know how much longer Carpenter has."

She gave a tight nod. "Come," she said. "Let's at least get there before the witching hour." She headed for the door before she looked down at her state of undress and caught herself. "I'd better change first."

"Maybe leave a message for your husband," Dimitri suggested.

She opened the door into the main shop. "We have an apartment above the shop. Wait here." She started up a set of stairs heading up to the living quarters.

"He has every right to punch me in the face," Dimitri mused.

"Let's hope we don't run into him, then," I said. But seriously, I understood that these guys wanted to protect us. They also needed to know when to let go. Aimee was a big girl. She understood the risks. "I didn't even know she was married," I added. "Does your husband know voodoo?" I called after her. Maybe he could help.

"He doesn't practice," she said, her voice trailing from the open apartment door upstairs. "But he has every reason to believe."

She returned wearing a loose-fitting neon green skirt, a hot-pink stretchy top, and white tennis shoes. She'd tied her hair back into an orange striped bandana and held a flashlight. "All set."

Dimitri frowned, as if he realized that protecting her would be a bigger job than he'd thought. I could understand his concern. If she were one of the biker witches, I would have told her to skip the flashlight. She'd glow in the dark all by herself. But I didn't say that because I was polite, and there was something I liked about the voodoo mambo.

She was comfortable in her own skin. I admired her confidence.

Or maybe it was simply that I needed her.

"Let's bring this just in case," she said, plucking two stones, a candle, and a red cloth bundle from her altar.

"Sounds great." I'd stick with my switch stars.

We headed out the back, and Aimee locked her door. Dimitri's frown deepened as she motioned us into a dark corridor on the other side of the alley. I hadn't noticed it before.

My husband drew me close. "Short cut?" he asked.

"The best way," she said, moving first through the narrow space. We followed close behind.

Laughter and conversation from the party crowd filtered from the surrounding streets, making the corridor feel even more secluded.

Dimitri slipped his hand into mine. "You've done this before," he said to the voodoo mambo as the path emptied into another alley.

She tossed a glance over her shoulder. "It's a long story. You wouldn't believe me if I told you."

We followed the back streets and alleys until we came to Basin Street.

Sweat trickled down the back of my neck as the white stone walls of a graveyard rose up in front of us.

St. Louis Cemetery Number One used to be located at the outskirts of the city, which now meant the edge of the French Quarter. The cemetery closed its gates at dusk, for safety's sake. Most people assumed that meant the prevention of criminal activity. But knowing what I did of the other side, I'd be willing to bet other things went down in the dark cemetery at night.

"I hear it's a maze in there," I said quietly.

"I know the way," she said, leading us past the front entrance. A simple wrought-iron cross topped the tall gate. I paused to look in on the aboveground tombs, pearly white in the light of the moon. "Stay close to me, no matter what you see in there. There are more than one hundred thousand departed souls resting inside those walls. Most are dead and gone. But there are some who practiced voodoo and their power calls to me. I'm never truly alone in there."

"Great," Dimitri said, eyeing the wall.

"This way," she said, hurrying to an area at the north edge where the streetlights were widely spaced and the side street deserted. Tall trees rose up on our side of the fence, their heavy canopies dripping over to the other side. She hitched a toe in the thick white stone wall like she'd done it dozens of times before.

Oh, who was I kidding? She probably had.

She found every nook and cranny until she crouched at the top of the wall. Then she paused, her features clouding with worry. "I didn't think of how you—"

"No problem," I said, drawing on my power, willing it to lift me off the ground. There was something to be said for levitation, I decided, as I joined her on the top of the wall.

We both crouched low. "Nice trick," she said, without a trace of irony.

"Demon slayer," I said. No sense hiding it.

Dimitri found hand and toeholds I hadn't even noticed and soon joined us at the top. Together, we looked out over tangled rows upon rows of graves. No wonder they called it a city of the dead.

"Follow me." Aimee scooted her legs over the wall and leapt to the ground.

Dimitri motioned for me to go first, so I did, although I couldn't resist slowing my descent just a bit as I neared the ground on the other side. In any case, jumping sometimes made my knees hurt.

In one graceful leap, Dimitri was at my side. "You've gotten better at that."

"You should have seen me stick that landing in the swamp." It had been pure magic, or at least as close as I could get to it.

Aimee grinned. "I can see why Carpenter picked you two."

I couldn't help but return her smile. "I don't think he had much of a choice." At least as far as I was concerned.

"Come on," she said, getting her focus back. "Just because I've come here a lot doesn't mean it's safe to linger."

We left the shadow of the trees and kept our lights off for the time being. There was enough of a moon tonight and we didn't want to draw attention. Aimee moved almost silently and so did Dimitri and I as we wound through the crumbling monuments to the dead.

The place smelled like mold and concrete and the heat of the city. Wrought-iron gates with thick spikes hugged some of the white stone vaults, while others lay neglected, their plaster falling away to expose redbrick skeletons. Still others had sunk into the ground, their inscriptions worn and barely visible as earth swallowed them whole.

Entire extended families shared mausoleums separated by narrow pathways.

We passed a tomb coated in crumbling white marble, with a weeping angel over the doorway. It radiated power and darkness.

Aimee touched my arm to keep me moving. "We don't notice a thing," she said, as if failing to acknowledge it could somehow diminish its power.

That approach seemed to be working so far with the spirit in my head. I winced at myself for thinking of him and purposely cleared my thoughts.

Dimitri strode next to me, shoulders drawn back, focused on every detail of the cemetery.

"Lord, I missed you," I told him.

A slight grin tickled his lips. "So you showed me earlier."

"Up ahead," Aimee murmured over her shoulder. We took a hard left, and I knew immediately which grave was that of the Three Sisters. It stood at the end of a short, dead-end row. The tomb radiated malice and death, as if it could infect the living with merely a brush or a touch. Maybe it could.

There was nothing remarkable about the stone itself—plain white, topped with a simple slanted roof. It was better kept than most of the others, with white paint and a well-maintained exterior. Vases set into the path on either side held fresh blood-red roses twined with strands of pearls and feathers. More flowers scattered the ground in front of the entrance, along with offerings of rum and cigarettes.

The name on the etched gray stone read *Pade*.

I gave an involuntary shudder.

"Pade's mother was a powerful dark bokor," Aimee said quietly, as if her words themselves could summon her. "His grandmother and his great-grandmother held great influence as well, but none so much as Mamma Pade. There are five generations in that crypt."

I glanced to Aimee, who stood with her arms over her chest, as if she couldn't get warm. "How many ancestors are we talking about in there?"

"I don't know. Sometimes servants and followers are buried with the family…if they've shown enough loyalty."

Dimitri stiffened next to me. "I wonder what that entails."

I'd seen it firsthand.

"Every family member adds power." Aimee paused. "Feel that spiky energy coming off it?"

I raised a hand over the stone. The jabbing power tore at my palm like a thousand tiny, piercing arrows.

"It's probably cursed," she said pragmatically. "And before you ask, I can't lift a generational curse in an evening."

I hadn't asked. Damn. "Carpenter said this was important." It had better be. We could be sacrificing a lot.

Aimee looked like she might cry. "He may get in over his head sometimes, but he knows how to get out."

He was asking a heck of a lot in the process.

"What exactly is there between you and Carpenter?" Dimitri asked. It was an uncomfortable question, and I prepared myself for an answer I didn't want to hear. Then again, we needed to know what skin she had in the game.

If his question surprised her, she didn't show it. The voodoo mambo lifted her chin. "He's my half-brother."

I sighed. "He hadn't told me."

She looked grimmer than I'd ever seen her. "He's a very private person."

That was an understatement.

She watched me carefully. "You said you could stop Osse Pade."

"I'm trying," I assured her. I reached out and forced myself to touch the front of the tomb. It was freezing cold, even on this sultry night. The energy cut at my hand. The surface felt as if it were pulsing.

I ran my hands over the stone blocking the entrance, looking for a way inside.

Dimitri took my hand and gently lifted away. "You're not going in. I am."

I appreciated the sentiment, but in this case, he wasn't the right one for the job. "We don't know if you're equipped to deal with this kind of evil." His griffin power drew its strength from goodness and light. Osse Pade dealt in blood and death. "I've tasted Osse Pade's power before, in the swamp. I survived."

His grip on my hand tightened. "Maybe you just got lucky."

"Nobody's going in," Aimee said. "A curse like this can kill you. We can get what we need from here."

"I hope you're right." Whatever was inside the tomb called to me. It wanted me. I ran my hands over the stone once more. I felt the energy surge, the pull of power.

A cloud moved over the moon and the cemetery plunged into even deeper darkness.

I inspected the edge of the entrance. Sweat tickled the base of my neck. I found a fingerhold near the top and, deeper inside, a lever.

"Be careful," Aimee hissed.

The time for that was long past.

"Here." I handed Dimitri my Maglite. I pressed the lever and braced myself as the stone fell away from the entrance to the tomb.

Dimitri shone the light inside. The beam illuminated age-blackened walls. Cobwebs and unidentifiable filth clung to the corners and to the sloped ceiling. It smelled of dirt, rot, and death.

He slanted the light toward the floor and I stiffened. "Look," I said, barely above a whisper.

"Sweet Mother," Dimitri hissed.

The tomb stood empty. The bones were gone.

Chapter Fifteen

Aimee edged in close to me, wide eyed. "What happened to the bones?"

My blood ran icy cold. "Why would anyone take dead bodies?"

Aimee stood stock-still. "Spells. Potions."

Dimitri frowned. "Curses."

I had a feeling it was more than that. The spirit in the house had teased me with it:

All blood is not the same.

All bones are not the same.

I felt him stir in the back of my mind. No doubt he wanted me to return for the next piece of the puzzle. I didn't think that was such a hot idea.

Aimee touched my cheek softly, turning my face towards hers. "What was that?"

"I don't know what you mean," I said, pulling away from her touch.

She wasn't swayed. "I think you do."

"It's not important," I told her.

Oh, Elizabeth. His voice sounded in my head. *How deeply you wound me.*

"Let's talk about what's going on with these bones," I said. We couldn't do anything about the spirit right now. Carpenter was another matter. I forced myself to stay focused. "Osse Pade has a little trophy display back at the funeral parlor. Shelves full of bones, with pictures and mementos." It had been creepy enough as a voodoo display. "I didn't realize it was anyone he knew."

"It might not be," Aimee said, her fingers twining around the gris-gris bag hanging from a cord around her neck.

"She's right," Dimitri said. "You're jumping to conclusions. Let's think logically…"

He hadn't seen the voodoo bokor like I had. "Osse Pade jumped off the logic train a long time ago." But I could see the point. At one time, I wanted everything to fit into neat little boxes. Now I knew you sometimes had to go on gut instinct, and right now, this was the only theory that made sense. "Osse Pade is all wrapped up in his ancestors."

"That is part of voodoo," Aimee conceded. "Our loved ones are always with us on the spirit plane."

"I get that, but this is different. He practically worships them." Then it hit me. "Carpenter suspected. That's why he had us come out here. The missing bones must have something to do with what they have planned for your brother." If so, there was only one way to protect him. "We need to get those bones." It would slow them down, at least for now.

"Again," Dimitri said, with a quick glance to the empty grave.

"Oh my goddess," Aimee whispered, her hands fluttering around her neck like birds. "What do you expect me to do? I can't break into a funeral parlor."

I liked where she was going with that, but, "We won't do any breaking and entering," I assured her. Not with the congregation I saw there tonight. "We'll sneak in."

She went a little pale at the suggestion. "We?"

"Me and Dimitri," I corrected. We'd rocked her world enough for one night. And we might need her later. "Plus, I have only one extra Sneak spell."

She groaned at that, but she didn't argue.

Dimitri's gaze heated. "Glad we tested out the Sneak spell earlier."

I nudged him. "That's one of the things I love about you. You're very thorough."

He grinned and planted a kiss on my forehead. "Let's finish up here."

"I'll do it," I said, moving past him. I closed the tomb with a grunt while Aimee stared at me.

"You're serious about this," she said.

"As a heart attack." I wiped my hands on my pants, trying to ignore the way they tingled. And trying to forget the way that one Sneak spell hadn't exactly worked out for me. We'd have to keep it close and hope for the best.

She looked a little shaky. "I can't believe I'm doing this." I didn't know if she meant the tomb breaking and entering or the funeral parlor trip we were about to take.

Either way, "I feel we're getting a lot done tonight," I told her.

She stared at me as if I'd just asked her on a satanic picnic. "My brother is still in a hexed circle; Osse Pade's ancestors are missing; you made me peek into the cursed tomb of a voodoo queen"—her voice kept going up and up—"I'm hoping to heaven my husband didn't come home yet, while you two are about to break into a voodoo funeral parlor."

"Like I said. Productive night."

Dimitri gave me a kiss on the forehead and we set out, ignoring the way Aimee got a little huffy on the way out of the cemetery. She might not be used to the way we operated, but I knew she was in it for the long run. That was good, because I had a feeling we'd need her.

✝✝✝

We didn't speak again until we were over the cemetery wall and deep into the back alleys leading to Royal Street. Crowds of revelers shouted in the distance and jazz filtered from the clubs.

Aimee led the way, darting around parked motorcycles and trashcans, easing us from one back way to the next.

I tried to keep my mind off the spirit. It only served to draw him.

When you're not thinking of me, you're thinking of me.

Damn it.

Don't worry. I like it.

"Lizzie?" Dimitri wrapped an arm around me. "Tell me what's going on."

"It's talking to me again," I said. "The spirit from the house. As soon as my mind even goes there..."

"Then don't," he said quickly. I could tell it scared the heck out of him. "Think of something else."

Easier said than done.

The voodoo mambo glanced over her shoulder at me and made a sign of the cross.

"Don't you start, too," I warned. "You two aren't doing anything to take my mind off this." In fact, at this rate they were going to turn me into a magical hypochondriac.

She sighed and reached into her pocket, drawing out the tied red bundle she'd taken from her altar. "I'd gathered this for my anti-shoplifting spell, but let's use it now. It will give you strength." She folded open the cloth to reveal what appeared to be coffee grounds. "Bend over," she said, reaching up to sprinkle it over my head.

The spirit chuckled as she began to dust the dark grounds over me. But as she emptied her bundle, I could hear his voice fade.

"What is it?" Dimitri asked.

"Grave dirt," she said, tucking the red cloth back into her pocket. "From consecrated ground, not the place we just visited," she said, as if there was a difference.

Who was I kidding? I'd bet there was.

"It drives away bad or simply mischievous spirits," she said softly. Then to both of us, she added, "I saw a lot of activity down the street earlier tonight. Lots of people going in and out of that funeral parlor."

"Same when we stopped by your place." I had a feeling my hunch was right.

Dimitri took my hand as we traveled two more streets, then paused at the edge of an alleyway. I'd lost my bearings for a moment, which was unlike me.

We were farther down than I thought, past Aimee's voodoo shop and right across the street from Osse Pade's funeral parlor.

The sign out front remained dark, but lights blazed from the windows. We watched a guard open the door for a pair of church members, a man and a woman, dressed in white. The security leader had ditched the purple face paint, and he wore a simple white shirt, but I recognized the man who had tried to grab me outside Carpenter's hut.

Four more guards stood outside: two by the front entrance, one by each end of the storefront. I saw a half dozen more on the roof.

"Jackpot." I grinned.

Dimitri squeezed my hand.

"Look at those armed guards," she protested. "This should not excite either one of you."

"It means we're in the right spot to mess things up for him," Dimitri murmured.

"Plus, I have biker witch magic." It was all falling into place.

Of course, this was usually the point where sparks flew and the whole thing exploded.

The crowning glory was when my emerald necklace warmed and began to glow. Aimee watched slack-jawed as the metal chain went liquid and snaked down my neck and chest. "It's defensive," I told her, by way of explanation, as the liquid bronze formed a chest plate that reached down to my leather bustier. The teardrop shaped emerald sat squarely in the middle.

Showtime.

Well, almost. I dug around in my pocket and came out with a round, blue orb with sparkles inside. Sneak spell. I handed it to Dimitri. "Put this in your pants." It was the tightest place I could think where it would stay put and be close to his skin.

Lucky spell.

"I never should have answered my door," Aimee muttered as Dimitri turned his back to her and slid the spell into place.

"Jam it in there good," I told him, double-checking mine to make sure it was still there.

Snug as a bug in a rug.

Aimee furrowed her brow. "You really think you can get in there? Those people are in suits and dresses and you look like you've been combing your hair with twigs."

Yeah, well, she looked like a rainbow, but I wasn't about to make fun of her wardrobe choices. "You were the one who poured dirt over my head," I reminded her.

Dimitri, as usual, stayed on task. "We've tested the on-the-body Sneak spell," he assured her.

"With mind-blowing results," I added.

She seemed to calm at that.

"You can be our backup in case things go bad. You don't have to go in. In fact..." I grabbed a pen out of my utility belt. "Here." I took her hand and wrote Grandma's cell number on her palm. "Call the biker witches if we're not out in an hour."

"Don't trust anyone you meet in there," Aimee instructed.

"Have you had dealings with any of them?" I asked, curious. The voodoo community had to be small.

Aimee didn't answer directly. "I looked in the window," she said. "There's a twisted veve on the floor of the lobby. It's designed to possess and control."

"I saw it," I said, glad I'd instinctively avoided it when I'd been inside.

Dimitri stood in the shadows at the corner of the alley, observing the street. "I just counted six more people going in."

I joined him. "Those are more church members," I said, recognizing the fire-eating woman from the ceremony in the swamp. She wore a white gown and was accompanied by three other women.

"Let's go," he said, ducking out of the alleyway. I kept pace beside him, marveling at his smooth athletic grace and the way he maneuvered in behind two older men as they crossed the street toward the funeral parlor.

He was a natural at this sneak stuff. Dimitri winked at me as the guard opened the door and we passed into the funeral parlor with the group. Bodies crowded the lobby, cloying incense thick in the air. The room buzzed with the chants of the faithful.

This time, rich silk flags decorated the walls. They pictured dancing skeletons, twining snakes, and flaming hearts struck through with swords.

Festive.

We stuck to the edges, avoiding the swirling white designs on the floor of the lobby.

The Sneak spells seemed to be working. The worshippers focused on the large wooden altar at the back, crowded with candles and bones of the dead. They spoke in Haitian Creole, their words thick with emotion and need.

Pran dlo nan je nou Et pran zosman nou
Mettre pou lavi ki pwòp pa nou

In my mind, I could almost *hear* the translation. It was one of the niftier demon-slayer powers. At least for a geek like me. I could translate script as well. I concentrated and let the words come:

Take our tears and take our bones
Bring to life what is our own

Holy smokes. "They're praying for resurrection."

Dimitri visibly paled. "Never a dull day."

I drew ahead as we neared the doorway that led to the courtyard. When Osse Pade had taken me back there, I'd seen nothing but a simple open air space with rows of chairs, a rough altar, and a platform for a coffin.

When we slipped through the door this time, I had no idea what to think.

"Bodies," Dimitri whispered.

"You're not kidding."

Four rows of tables stretched across the courtyard. Followers dressed in white huddled over them, assembling bones. Each table held a skeleton. One skull, one pelvis, assorted arm bones and fingers and toes.

They were putting everyone back together again, like some twisted version of Humpty Dumpty.

Thick red candles flickered from sconces on the walls. We slipped into the shadows near the far left corner.

Osse Pade stood in the doorway to his private sanctuary. Black and white paint streaked his face and chest, mimicking a skeleton. He lovingly held what appeared to be a human skull. His fingers caressed the forehead and lingered over the empty eye sockets. "Can you feel her?" he purred. "She wants to come to us."

A nearby male priest appeared nervous, overwhelmed. "It is difficult, my bokor. We cannot sense her like you can." He bowed his head quickly back to his work. "The remains are old."

"Age doesn't matter," Osse Pade said, cradling the skull as he observed the half-completed skeletons. "You must go by what you feel. We trust in magic above all things."

He swept a hand over the remains nearest to him and a long thigh bone began rattling on the table. It shook all on its own, bumping against the tangle of bones piled on all sides.

The voodoo bokor smiled. "Mamma." He gently stroked the bone before plucking it from the others. "You see? All bones are not the same."

My palms began to sweat. It was the same thing the spirit had said to me.

He removed his mother's thigh bone and lovingly placed it into a pink coffin at the front. "There."

Dimitri stiffened next to me. "They're putting Mamma Pade back together."

Sweet puppies.

I'd seen a lot of things as a demon slayer that I never would have believed before I'd gotten my powers. This was right up there.

The bokor turned, his fingers stroking the skull. "Mamma's bones, they call to me. Just as they will call to you. You must let yourselves hear her. Open yourselves to her power. Let her strength seep into you. It's the only way we can do what needs to be done."

"Why?" I hissed, my words barely audible. "Why do they want Mamma back together?" I thought back to the alligator in the swamp. How he'd put a soul into it.

A line of sweat trickled down Dimitri's cheek. "You said it yourself," Dimitri murmured. "Resurrection."

Like the chicken in the swamp. That thing had a body. These remains, these bones were well and truly dead. "This isn't Night of the Living Demon Slayer," I protested.

"Think again." Dimitri stuck close to me, his breath coming hard. "Theoretically, reanimation is possible."

Anyone who tried would surely be doomed. But Osse Pade had already gone down that road. I cringed as the bokor kissed his mother's skull.

"Careful, now. Slowly," he said as his followers prayed over a body. Two vertebrae began twitching, along with a finger bone. "We don't want her mixed up with Aunt Ceila or anybody else. Trust in magic above all things," he repeated like a mantra.

They carried the shivering vertebrae to the pink coffin.

"We've got to stop this," Dimitri hissed.

I agreed. We couldn't let this happen. But I had no idea how to put a halt to it.

Think. We couldn't let them use Carpenter to raise up Mamma. For all I knew, they may mean to kill him while they did it.

Of course, they couldn't raise Mamma without a few key parts.

"I'm going to steal her head."

"What?" Dimitri barked, a little too loud. The priests and priestesses of the cult turned and stared into the shadows where we hid.

"They won't see me until I'm on top of them." And it would keep them from raising Mamma.

Of course it would require a direct assault on the bokor, who murmured to the head as he lingered near the coffin. At this point, I wouldn't be surprised if he started singing it lullabies.

My husband clenched his jaw, as if he couldn't quite believe he was doing this. "There's another way," he murmured. "Follow my lead."

Chapter Sixteen

This was why I'd missed my dear husband. Sure, I had no idea what he was about to pull, but I knew it would be epic. And for our sakes, it had better work.

Dimitri and I kept close to the wall as we snuck up the side of the room toward Osse Pade. We slipped behind a huddled group of men and women in white. They rocked their bodies forward and back with a desperation only matched by their harsh, moaning chants.

Sulu oh madre
Sulo oh loa fete
Sulu oh madre
Sulo oh loa fete

I hovered so close I feared the edge of their dresses would brush my boots. Dimitri kept his arms and hands flat against the wall and zeroed in on a spot ahead of us. He glanced back at me and gave a quick nod as if to ask, "Ready?"

Oh, yes.

He broke from behind the worshippers and dashed directly into Osse Pade's office.

No one saw him. I couldn't believe it. That was either the dumbest move or the smartest. And the witches definitely needed to brew up some more Sneak spells.

I shoved off the wall and bolted after him, running headlong for the arched wooden doorway. The chanting rose up on all sides of me. The cloying scent of incense

NIGHT OF THE LIVING DEMON SLAYER   143

invaded my nose and stung my eyes. I held my breath against it as I ducked into Osse Pade's sanctuary.

Dimitri caught me against his chest. He was a rock wall in the blackness and he wasn't even trying to hide. His eyes flashed orange, then yellow as the adrenaline coursed through him. Yes, he was a man, but he was also a shape-shifter and he was never more animal then when he was primed for battle.

My body tensed, ready for the fight.

He could see in the dark much better than I could. When he didn't move against the next threat, I took my hand off my switch stars.

We'd gone undetected. For now, we had the advantage.

Just outside, the cult members chanted and held their blades and torches aloft. The bones lay naked and exposed. Osse Pade looked like a man possessed as he stroked his mamma's skull.

Then he jerked and stared right at our hiding place. My heart raced. We needed time...for what, I didn't know. I was so tempted to run up and grab the skull from him, but then where would we go? We'd have no escape. There were too many of them.

My husband gripped me by the shoulders. Wordlessly, he tucked me behind him. I let him because I trusted him. He seemed to have a plan.

Then he grabbed hold of the shelf along the wall, the long one that held the bones and mementos and bits of bodies that Osse Pade treasured. With a mighty heave, he brought it crashing down onto the floor.

What the hell? I leapt back as glass, bone, and debris smashed to pieces. It scattered, striking my boots and tripping me as I beat a hasty retreat.

"Are you insane?" I screeched. My volume certainly didn't matter anymore.

He didn't even react to my outrage. "Steady," he murmured, bracing for a fight as the bokor ran straight for us, barking orders to his machete-wielding bodyguards.

Dimitri raised his hands in front of him. "No switch stars," he ordered. "Now!"

Osse Pade burst through the doorway. Dimitri grabbed him by the shoulders and used the bokor's own momentum to drag him inside. He yanked the skull from Pade and tossed it to me before gripping the bokor's shoulders once more and using him as a battering ram. He shoved the furious leader past the guards crowding the doorway and out into the courtyard.

I caught Mamma's head. I stared down at the skull in my hands. The jaw rattled and I hoped to God it wasn't alive.

We were never going to get this thing out of here.

Just outside, Dimitri crashed down on top of Osse Pade, knocking down two of the tables, scattering bones. A half-dozen guards piled on top of him like linebackers. He was down.

Or was he?

Dimitri let out a low beastly growl and I knew exactly what my griffin had in mind.

The pile of guards shifted and rose straight up under Dimitri's rapidly expanding form. His shirt tore. Thick lion's fur raced up his arms and over his back. Red, blue, purple, and green feathers formed wings as his bones shifted and his body grew to the size of a truck.

Dimitri unfurled his enormous wings, the feathers tipped in gold. He clipped another table, sending it crashing down, toppling several guards with it. He threw back his eagle head and called out a sharp battle cry.

He bent his massive lion's body low to the ground and I dashed straight for him. His fur felt smooth and warm, like a cat's. There was no way to straddle his back. It was too wide. So I climbed on with my legs over his shoulders and my fingers twined into the rough fur at his neck. I tucked the skull under my arm, ignoring the way its jaws snapped at my skin.

I took an extra second to tighten my grip. "I'm on! Let's go!" Griffins were like Ferraris. They could go from zero to two hundred in about five seconds flat.

As ready as I was, my head still jerked back as Dimitri lurched skyward, stunning the dazed guards. His claws scraped the air inches above their heads.

The magic in the air singed my cheeks and body.

Mamma's skull struggled against my grip, but I held on tight. She wasn't getting away. Not now.

I felt like I'd hitched a ride on a rocket as we jettisoned out of the courtyard and up into the night.

We did it. We'd actually pulled this off. I grinned hard, loving this, loving *him*.

Dimitri's shoulders shuddered underneath my thighs and he gave a sharp cry as we slammed into a solid wall of voodoo. The heat of it blazed through me. We jerked backward and plunged straight down.

CHAPTER SEVENTEEN

We landed hard on the stone tile. Dimitri had his feet under him. He was conscious. That was about all I could find on the bright side. I rolled off his back and drew a switch star, striking the barrel of the pistol aimed at my husband's head. It shaved the end off, rumpling the metal, making it impossible to fire.

Then six more guards aimed guns at us.

So much for trusting in magic.

I tried to block Dimitri as he curled to his side and began to shift. He was at his most vulnerable during the change. He had to be hurt or in severe pain to be doing it now in front of this crowd. We'd hit the ground with bone-jarring force and he'd taken the brunt of the blow.

Feathers in blue, green, and purple folded over on themselves. He shimmered as his lion's body morphed to reveal a broad, muscled back, lean legs, and a bloodied floor underneath.

Damn.

Within seconds he was on his feet, naked and unarmed. He clutched a hand to his side.

Are you okay? The question screamed through my head, but I didn't dare ask it out loud. It would do him no good for us to show weakness.

He appeared dazed and unsteady. I reached for him, but a guard blocked my way.

Dimitri gave me a reassuring nod that turned into more of a grimace as we were dragged forward in front of the fuming bokor.

The burly guard with the feather necklace snatched the skull out of my grip. Another dragged my hands behind my back, making it impossible for me to go for my weapons.

"Place her in the casket," Osse Pade ordered. For a heart-stopping moment, I thought he meant me. "Let her rest...at least for now." He smiled, drawing his hands together as his goon took his mother's skull to join the rest of her bones.

Osse Pade's straight white teeth gleamed. The white skull paint crackled against his skin as he turned back to us. He walked a small circle around Dimitri and me.

His followers shrank back and bowed their heads in reverence.

The bokor stopped directly in front of my husband, appearing entirely too pleased to see him. Guards held Dimitri on each side, rooting him to the spot. He swayed and I hoped he was playing it up. We were in big trouble if he was as shell-shocked as he looked.

"A griffin." The bokor's dark eyes sparkled with interest. "I could never have imagined *you*."

Dimitri glared at him, refusing to be baited into offering him anything.

Osse Pade touched a calloused finger to my husband's broad chest. His nails were long, like a woman's. "When this is all over, I'm sure Mamma will find you quite tasty." His finger trailed down Dimitri's exposed sternum.

I had no idea what he meant, but I had a pretty good inkling I never wanted to find out. I must have made some sort of noise because the bokor directed a soulless smile at me.

"I'll even let you watch, little demon slayer." He considered me, as if deciding on what kind of special treat I deserved. "You'll make a great enforcer. I never believed in your kind, either, but I'll bet you could show me a thing or two."

I drew back as far as I could from him. "I'd have to be insane to work for you."

He tilted his head. "That could be arranged." He watched me, as if he could pick apart my power that way. "I have enemies and voodoo takes time." His gaze found the switch stars at my belt. "I'll bet your weapons are quicker. I don't even have to hurt you." He drew close, his spicy breath warming my cheek. "How well you work for me determines how much I do or don't slice off your griffin."

I refused to react. I would not show this waste of a human being how his words cut me to the core.

The biker witches would come. We had backup. We just had to wait until they realized we were in trouble. Then pray they did better against the bokor than we had.

"You have hope," he said, as if he could read my mind. "I like that. It means you're a fighter, like me." His congenial tone evaporated. "But let me make one thing clear, as soon as I raise Mamma, she and I will be unstoppable. Joining her body with her soul will give her life. The necromancer's blood will make her immortal."

The guard with the feather necklace approached. "He's here."

Osse Pade's mouth tipped at the corners. "Bring him in."

Two guards dragged Carpenter through the wide archway. He was shirtless, bloody and bruised. He wore the same black pants from the night he was taken. Thick ropes secured his hands behind his back and snaked up his back to form a noose around his neck.

The crowd recoiled as he lurched and tried to throw off the guards. He gurgled as they tightened the noose behind him.

"Kneel." The guard behind me shoved me to my knees on the stone floor and secured my arms with a rough rope binding. He wrapped the remaining length around my neck.

It bit into my skin and squeezed dangerously tight. I struggled for breath.

Don't panic.

They bound Dimitri the same way. We shared a glance. I didn't know what we were going to do. We had to escape, but I couldn't get to my weapons. I couldn't overpower the guard at my back through sheer physical strength, even if I wasn't tied and half-strangled.

A man in a yellow tunic approached the front of the room where we stood. I recognized him as the same man who'd slashed his belly with a knife at the ceremony in the swamp. "It's not time yet," he said, twisting his hands together. "We still need to find the rest of her ribcage." He eyed the coffin, nervously drumming his fingertips. "And a pinky toe."

Osse Pade glared down at the man. "I don't care about a pinky toe." He lifted his arms to the sky. "We raise her now!"

Excited shouts erupted from the congregation, lyrical exclamations in a language I didn't immediately understand. Then it hit me.

They were calling for her.

Manman nou! Manman Pade!

Our mother. Mother Pade.

"We will bring her home to you!" Pade announced.

Drums began to pound. They took up a slow, steady rhythm, mimicking a human heartbeat.

I twisted my wrists, fighting the knots that bound them. They'd tied me tight.

Okay.

I worked my arms sideways, ignoring the uncomfortable stretch in my shoulders. There had to be some way to catch a rope on the top of my switch stars. If I could just…force it.

The guards dragged Carpenter by the neck toward the wax-stained sacrificial altar in front of the casket.

My left shoulder screamed and my eyes watered with pain as I tried to reach my switch stars. It wasn't working.

Frick.

Then I remembered the small, bald creature who lived in the back pocket of my demon-slayer utility belt. I'd inherited Harry along with the belt. He refused to come out and liked to bite my fingers. Hard. Maybe he just mistook them for the occasional bacon slice or pizza crust I'd sneak him.

Come on, Harry. Now was the time to make it up to me.

I reached for the flap of Harry's hideaway with my fingertips. "Hey, little guy," I murmured. I felt the sting of his teeth and winced. "Good boy." I rolled my shoulders back and felt Harry latch onto the rope. I jiggled it and felt him bite down harder.

Atta boy.

Of course, the rope was thick. And from the glimpses I'd gotten, I'd say Harry was about the size of a small hamster.

I wriggled my wrists and heard Harry growl as he attacked with added vehemence.

We were running out of time.

Two guards lashed Carpenter to the stone altar like an animal brought to sacrifice. Women in white rushed forward with thick candles and placed them around the struggling necromancer. Another approached with fire and sent flames leaping up over the thick, red wax.

Aye-yay-yay! Voices erupted all around us.

The bokor stood behind Carpenter with his back to the casket. He swayed to the beat of the drums, eyes closed, arms outstretched, as if he were entering a trance.

"We beseech the dark loa, the mother of death! Come to us!" Pade called. The music changed. The drums stuttered out a staccato beat and the people screamed with abandon, thrashing their bodies. "We call our ancestors. Come to us!"

The air grew heavy and I could feel the spirits descend over the crowded courtyard. Their voices rushed over us and whispered in the corners. They twisted in the smoke from the fire.

Pade slowly tugged at the leather strap around his neck and pulled out a pendant tied with yellow cloth and lashed with sticks and feathers. Oh boy. It looked exactly like the trap Carpenter had tried to bring to me. An object inside the bag quivered and I knew who it had to be.

Mamma.

"I've got you," the bokor coo'ed. He drew the bag off his neck and broke it over the coffin.

I felt for the rope at my back. Harry had about half of it chewed through. He clamped down on my pointer finger and I fought back a curse. I shook him off and felt the warm blood bubble up.

Come on. I baited him with the rope again, scared when he didn't latch on right away. Then I felt the weight of his bite and the shake of his head as he attacked with lusty vigor.

Osse Pade bent over the casket and drew out a long stick topped with a skull. I'd seen that before, in the swamp. He'd used it to strike the chicken dead.

He whipped it toward the crowd, laughing as they cowered. "Are you afraid of death?" he taunted. "I'm not."

Yeah. Because he was insane.

He pointed the skull at Carpenter, who lay on the altar, struggling. "He's the one who should be afraid."

A harsh wind tore through the courtyard, whipping at the candles lining the walls, scattering flecks of blood-red wax. It spattered over the congregants, wetting their skin, burning. The people swayed and clung to each other— some crying, others silent—as a dark power seeped into the courtyard like a living thing.

A sick crackling noise rose from the casket.

The bokor's eyes opened wide as he stared into the pink coffin. "Mamma's back!" His glee abruptly vanished. "Bring me the blade."

A woman in white rushed to the front and prostrated herself as she offered up a machete as long as my arm.

I lunged, shoving my wrists against my bonds. The ropes held. The guard behind me yanked me up by the noose, the thick rope cutting into my neck, choking me. My eyes watered. I gasped for air.

"Let her breathe!" Dimitri ordered. I barely heard, terrified, as my ears rang and my vision swirled.

I felt a rough yank at the rope around my neck and the wet on my cheeks as I sucked in a deep lungful of air. I raised my head just in time to see Osse Pade slice the machete down onto Carpenter's chest.

He gasped out a cry. Blood bubbled up from his abdomen and ran freely down his sides.

No telling how deep they'd cut him this time. If they'd bleed him out.

And I could do nothing but watch.

Osse Pade tilted a gold cup to catch the necromancer's blood. The flow surged with each grasping beat of Carpenter's heart. The drums mimicked the pounding. The cup overflowed, the blood sluicing down onto the floor.

We watched, horrified, as Osse Pade raised the chalice high and poured the blood over Mamma. It splashed wetly over her bones.

He clutched the empty, bloody cup, his entire body shaking. "We call to you, loa!" His eyes were wild as he stared down into the coffin. "We call to the mother of death!"

Was Carpenter even breathing? He'd turned a sickly gray, and his head lolled to the side. But his blood still flowed, slower now, dripping down into the drain on the floor.

"The mother of death...it's got to be Mamma," Dimitri muttered beside me. I hoped to God he was wrong.

All I could think about was Mamma's black soul seeping into blood-drenched bones on pink satin. Then back to that dead, twisted body of the chicken back in the swamp, sprawled in the dirt.

How its feathers, soaked in blood, had begun to twitch.

The drums struck hard and fast, in a heavy unnatural beat. Pade raised his arms to the blackened sky. "We call you back from spirit!" His chest heaved. Sweat beaded his forehead as he intoned, "Come be flesh and blood once more!"

A skeletal hand grasped the side of the casket.

Sweet mother.

A wind whipped through the courtyard, causing skin to flutter against bone. Veins snaked down her fingers. Tendons grasped together.

Osse Pade cried tears of joy. Carpenter bled. The altar candles ran with thick red wax. I stared in horror as skin stretched and grew over the once-dead hand.

No. Not once dead. *Still* dead. His mother couldn't be alive.

She couldn't.

Even after all I'd seen, after all I'd done, I still couldn't believe it.

The coffin shook and creaked. I watched in terror as a half-formed corpse rose from the silk bed. White eyeballs bulged in hollow sockets. Her bare jaw opened and closed, the tendons working, the teeth and bone exposed. Leathery skin blew loosely over high cheekbones. Thick arteries roped down her neck. They pulsed with blood. With life.

She turned her head and stared directly at me.

CHAPTER EIGHTEEN

Pallid gray skin stretched and grew over the bones thrusting from her cheeks. It sank into her eye sockets, making the whites bulge.

All at once, her gaze sharpened. Her top lip drew up as she studied me.

There was intelligence in that stare. Her brain might be half-rotted or, hell, for all I knew it was fresh and pink, but there was no doubt Mamma Pade was back.

As far as what she wanted with me…I had a sick feeling I was about to find out.

She held out a hand and let Osse Pade assist her from her coffin.

I struggled once more to free my wrists, knowing it was useless.

Mamma took one creaking step down from the viewing stage, then another, her gait unsteady, her limbs swinging. She was bald, naked, her left ribcage hollowed out and missing bones. The skin healed over muscle, leaving oozing trails of blood in its wake.

Instinctively, I drew back, the noose around my neck tightening, leaving me gasping for breath.

Osse Pade fluttered behind her. One of his assistants brought him a green robe that he draped over her shoulders. She ignored him and advanced on me.

Her son turned and began issuing orders to his followers. "Go get her silk slippers as well. And a chair. She may want to sit."

Ha. I didn't think Mamma Pade was slowing down anytime soon.

She drew uncomfortably close to me, her stale breath making my stomach roil. Her left eye socket hadn't closed and I could see down to the bone.

Her breath sounded like wind through rocks, rough and grinding. "A slayer," she said on an exhale, as if speaking was still foreign to her. Hell, walking should have been as well. Not to mention seeing, breathing, and…touching. She ran a skeletal finger over my cheek. I could feel the darkness in her, the pure black of her soul.

My throat tightened as she turned to Dimitri. She swiped a rough tongue over thinly formed lips. "And a toy."

"Let me go and I'll help you," I whispered, hoping to God that her son hadn't heard. Right now, I couldn't break free. I couldn't fight. But if I could somehow convince this corpse that I was of use to her, we might have a chance.

"Lizzie," Dimitri protested, his expression pained. He knew I didn't have a choice.

She stared at me, as if measuring my words. I held her gaze, ignoring the wriggling of something under her left eye, keeping my gaze steady as a fly emerged from under the skin and crawled over her exposed eyeball. The woman didn't blink and neither did I.

Her gaze moved to the noose at my neck and down to the ties that bound me.

"He's afraid I'll give you too much power," I murmured. "He wants to control you."

She laughed at that, a dry rusty sound. "I'll show you control, demon slayer."

She held up her hands and I heard the bones on the tables behind her begin to rattle.

A gasp erupted from the crowd.

Pade rushed to her, wide eyed. "They're not all sorted, Mamma."

She ignored him, her eyes feral, her jaw gritted.

"You're not strong enough yet," Pade insisted, his voice louder.

She thrust him away. He sprawled hard onto the steps before lurching to his feet, his features slack with surprise. Or perhaps fear.

The voodoo mamma reached for my throat and I gasped, prepared for her to squeeze. Her fingers dug into the soft skin of my neck as she threw off my noose. But she didn't untie me all the way.

I saw the black soul pulsing under the skin at the base of her throat. So close. I wanted to rip it out.

She turned and staggered toward the rows upon rows of tables, each holding a nearly complete skeleton.

Bones shook and clattered, and I about choked as I watched them begin to cling together. The spines rattled, the fingers twitched. The crowd gasped and slunk back as the bodies grew skin and sinew.

There had been no ceremony, no cutting of Carpenter. No black souls captured, no pretense of any kind.

Mamma slit her wrist open with her finger and a thin stream of blood bubbled up. Dry bones rubbed together. She was missing several teeth as she grinned. "Watch."

She dripped blood over the nearest corpse and it gasped, its chest thrusting out, its veins churning with life.

"She doesn't need us," Dimitri murmured. And he was right. Mamma had the power over life and death.

Mamma reached a hand to the corpse on the front table. A chill shuddered through me as it grasped her hand and sat up. It had the head of a youngish woman, with long stringy hair, fresh from the grave. It also had the shoulders of a muscular man, an arm of an elderly person, and a caved-in hole where the left shoulder should have been.

Mamma coaxed it off the table and it struggled to stand on uneven legs, the two knees not lining up as it lowered itself to bow to Mamma Pade.

Osse Pade rushed to her, mouth open as he stared at the Frankenstein zombie corpse made from his ancestors. "Stop. You don't need them," he pressed, growing desperate. "You have me."

Mamma wrinkled the leathery skin on her nose as she poured her blood out over the next corpse. "You're weak."

Pade looked as if he'd been slapped. "I raised you from the dead," he thundered.

She moved to the table after that. "You always were a suck-up." She dripped her bloody wrist over the last corpse as the entire row of bodies behind her began to twitch and groan.

Osse Pade ignored the insult as she moved to the next row.

"Let me sort them," Osse Pade pleaded. "Let me raise them with black souls. No more blood," he protested as she raised her dripping arm over the next corpse. "You can't make them immortal!"

She watched as it dripped over the bones, making them shudder. "That's the one thing I can't do," she said, frowning. "Yet," she added, glancing at me.

What the?—I struggled to figure out what she could mean. I didn't have power over the dead. I was just as mortal as the next person.

"These are my servants. They are my army," she added with relish as a man with half his face missing rose up from the table beside her.

"They can't reason. They can't obey," Osse Pade protested.

"They don't need to think," she growled, as if the mere idea offended her.

I tested my ropes. They held. Damn it.

Harry growled and struggled and I willed him to chew faster.

One by one, the dead stumbled from the tables and bowed before Mamma.

"This is no army," Pade spat, following her through the growing crowd of shambling corpses. "These are your powerful voodoo ancestors."

She moved on to the last row. "They will help me raise more."

Not if I could help it.

"Faster," I hissed to Harry. We needed to take them down.

Meanwhile, Osse Pade held her attention. "We can't hide this many," he protested. "People will see."

"We don't hide," Mamma lectured. "We rule."

Oh my word. I rolled my bound wrists, trying to work them free, earning a few angry nips in the process. She couldn't just let loose a horde of zombies on New Orleans.

Actually, she could.

"Come on," I whispered hotly as I felt my bonds slacken.

"Where is Andre?" she asked when she'd raised them all. Mamma whipped her head around, searching. The corpses around her twitched, their mismatched limbs making them gangly as they bobbed and swayed before her.

Pade's panic grew. He clutched his skull-tipped walking stick as if he could use it as a weapon against them.

"I didn't bury Andre with the family," Pade hissed. "I buried him in his wife's family crypt in St. Louis Cemetery Number One." He shoved off a corpse that stumbled against him. "He's not my true brother."

"He's my son," she thundered.

"Your favorite," Pade hissed. "But he is dead and *I* brought you back to life."

She appeared absolutely feral now, and I saw before Osse did that he'd made a grave mistake. He backed away, toward the altar that held a motionless Carpenter.

She followed, stalking the bokor. "You would do anything for your mother?"

"Yes," he said, standing before the altar without a shred of hesitation or guile.

She placed a hand on his head, and one on his shoulder. "Then die," she said, breaking his neck.

The drums silenced. The crowd waited. I could hear wet breathing and a few soft sobs as Mamma Pade raised her head to the crowd. "Do not worry, my sweetlings." She let her son fall, ignoring the sick crack of his head on the floor. "This time, I'll raise him to obey me."

I felt the ropes on my wrists drop and seized Harry before he could escape. He bit down on my knuckle, but I held him tight. With shaky hands, I pocketed the savage beast. Then I took a switch star and sliced through the ropes that held Dimitri. My fingers felt weak from lack of blood. Frick. I couldn't throw like this.

Mamma held her bloody wrist over her son's dead body and let the crimson liquid drip down over him.

"Do it," Dimitri said low in his throat. He didn't move. Didn't betray the fact that he was free. "End her," he urged.

It wasn't so simple. I didn't want to screw this up. I placed my hands behind my back as if they were still bound, rolling and stretching them until the feeling returned. I had one shot at this. One.

I got that they were distracted, but I couldn't let that force my hand.

Osse Pade gasped and sat up.

"There," she said, catching my eye.

Strength flooded back into my fingers. The nerves tingled with pain. They needed more time than Osse Pade to come back to life. But I couldn't wait. Not anymore.

She turned her attention back on her son. He slowly stood before her, as if waking from a deep sleep. His eyes appeared dazed and he stared right through the crowd and me. Mamma Pade stroked his hair. "There's my boy. Now you'll serve your mamma. I won't have you bickering with me or with Andre."

He stood, his neck lolling from his shoulders, the bones unable to hold it up. "Yes, Mother."

Now.

I drew a switch star and ran straight for Mamma. I drove it into her head as I reached into her neck with my other hand, ripping out the black soul. I flung it to the floor and crushed it under the heel of my boot, hoping to God that would kill it.

My switch star sliced straight through her skull, shattering bone and spraying brain matter. Osse Pade screamed. Mamma fell. And the dead turned toward me, snarling.

I couldn't kill them all. There were too many.

"This way!" Dimitri hollered as we started running.

CHAPTER NINETEEN

We burst down the side, past the startled church members, and skirted the edge of the lobby. Dimitri was stark naked, but we didn't care. Or maybe that was just me. At the last second, he grabbed a green and blue flag from the wall.

I kept a tight grip on him and we made a beeline past the guards and out the door.

The flag rippled behind him as we streaked across the street, taking refuge in the dark alley Aimee had shown us.

Thank heaven I still had that Sneak spell in my bra.

We were hidden. For now.

Dimitri's breath came in harsh pants. "You think you killed her?" he asked, working the silk flag around his waist. Damn. The man could make anything look good.

I turned my attention back to the funeral parlor, shocked we hadn't been followed. Yet. I wiped my bloody hands on my pants. "I pulled out the black soul. I've killed immortal demons with switch stars. And the undead alligator back in the swamp." It had to work. I didn't know what I'd do otherwise. "You get the witches. I'll stick here and pick off anything that tries to pursue us." It's not like he had any weapons on him anymore. With any luck, her undead followers were busy falling apart in there without her. "I'll stick here and make sure we got her."

He gave a quick nod. "I'll take the back way out of the alley and shift once I have the space."

"Perfect." He could travel faster when he was in griffin form. And if I needed to move, he'd be able to locate me thanks to the emerald I wore. I used to hate that. Now, I was damned grateful.

He gave me a fast, hard kiss. "Be careful."

"Always," I said, squeezing his hand tight before he slipped away into the darkness.

I turned back to observe the funeral parlor. The shadows around the lights had grown darker. Sparks of white rippled out over the center courtyard in peaks before descending over the worshippers inside. Most likely spirits of the dead. I shuddered to think of the kind of souls who would be at the call of a dark voodoo priestess like Mamma Pade.

But, no. She had to be gone.

It had gotten late. Gas streetlights cast uneven light. Sparse groups of tourists wandered farther down the block. I prayed they wouldn't come this way, especially when I saw a black hearse pull up in front of the building. It was drawn by four black horses. Their eyes glowed milky white and I could see the rib bones on one, where the papery skin hadn't grown all the way back. They snorted and dipped their heads.

Fuck a duck. Maybe I hadn't killed Mamma after all.

Osse Pade emerged, surrounded by members of the church. They flooded past him into the street. His eyes blazed hot and his head dipped at an unnatural angle. He opened the lobby door wide and bowed to Mamma. She'd survived. I didn't know how.

Her skull showed the damage from my switch star. I'd cleaved it in two pieces, straight down the center. Now, she held it together with a crown of beads, shot with a jeweled plume of pink and yellow feathers.

The halves fit together unevenly, with one eye socket higher than the other, the nose hole jagged, one side of her jaw lolling down. Her skin fluttered on both sides of the gash, exposing white bone.

There, at her neck, her black soul pulsed under a layer of papery skin.

I'd done my best and it hadn't worked. I'd barely slowed her down.

How in Hades was I going to kill her now?

The carriage swayed as she entered, followed by her son. The man in the yellow tunic climbed into the driver's box along with two of the women in white.

One thing was for certain: I couldn't let them get away.

My necklace hummed, the emerald stone warming against my neck. The bronze chain went liquid, snaking down my body as I watched the undead shamble from the funeral parlor.

Their snarls filled the night. I held my breath and waited as the soft metal glided down my side, over my hip. It twisted down my leg and settled on my left ankle, where it hardened right on my joint. Great. I tried to move my ankle and couldn't.

A group of tourists stopped down the block and started pointing at the corpses and the hearse, like it was some kind of show. Three girls rushed up to take pictures. The young blonde woman out front giggled with her friends, snapping selfies while a hissing man with a pearl necklace and an old woman's body lurched straight for her, arms out, teeth bared.

"No!" I rushed from my hiding place to save her from the monster. I gave it a boot to the chest and it hit the ground as the carriage clopped past us.

Mamma Pade watched out the window, her bulging white eyes locked on me.

"What are you? Crazy?" the girl demanded, while her friends continued to snap photos on their phones.

Oh my word. My mind reeled. I'd not only been caught by Mamma, but this was the first time I'd ever beheld supernatural phenomena that was visible to non-magical individuals.

"These people are dangerous," I warned, slapping away a girl taking video of the monster and me. They weren't even people, but I wasn't about to explain that for YouTube. "Get out of here!"

A hand grasped my ankle and the creature I'd shoved had his mouth open. He bit me, his teeth slamming against the enchanted bronze. I jumped back and smashed his head onto the pavement.

That's when the camera girls began to scream.

Bloody hell.

Pink brain matter oozed out from under my boot and I prayed to God that I'd killed the corpse.

"Stop it," I said, among the phone flashes.

Frick. Mamma was getting away. Her followers and the corpses trailed her down the street.

"Look." I dug into my utility belt and pulled out one of the Ziploc bags I'd packed for my original trip to this hellish place. Inside, living spells hovered, practically falling over themselves to escape. They refashioned themselves at will—flattening, lengthening, and twirling. "Here." I cursed under my breath at the top of the bag that would not open. I finally got it, my fingers closing around a shimmering corkscrew. I tossed it at camera girl. Hard. I launched two more at her friends. "Sick 'em," I ordered the gooey spells as they smacked the girls in the forehead.

Their expressions went blank.

Mind Wipers made you forget everything except what you most wanted to be. And they erased memory for a good five minutes before the event. I grabbed blondie's phone and started erasing the evidence.

The girl's anger disappeared and her face lit up. "I've always wanted to be a Kardashian!"

Lord almighty.

I handed her the phone back. By this time, my quarry was a good way down the block. I couldn't afford to lose them, but I had one more thing to do.

I drew a switch star and dashed back into the funeral parlor. The lobby stood empty. Hallelujah. I skirted the edges and entered the courtyard once more. Overturned tables littered the space, along with scattered pools of blood. Everyone had fled. Except for one poor soul.

Carpenter lay tied to the altar, struggling.

"Thank heaven you're still with us," I said, rushing toward him, using the blades of a switch star to cut him loose.

He winced, clutching his stomach, his muscles bunched and straining as he forced himself to sit. "Heaven has nothing to do with this."

"Hey, hey. Settle down." Truth be told, I was surprised he was still alive. The bleeding had stopped, but he looked terrible. "You need an ambulance."

"I've had worse." He waved me off. "And I heal faster than you." He struggled to his feet, chest heaving. "Right now, I need to figure out how he did it. How to stop her." The necromancer staggered toward Osse Pade's abandoned office. "Time is of the essence." He turned. "Why the hell are you still here?"

"I'm saving you," I insisted, feeling kind of dumb saying it.

He nodded, bracing a hand on the doorway to Osse Pade's office. "Go. Stop them as best you can. Hopefully, I can save *you*."

"Right." Mamma was getting away. I'd done what I could here. "Be safe," I said as I headed out of the abandoned funeral parlor. I made it outside, past the Mind Wiped tourists and toward the hearse that was still visible way down the street.

If Carpenter could figure out how to kill Mamma, if I could stop them in the meantime…we might just have a chance.

It was better than the alternative.

I took off after the undead funeral procession, walking funny with the bronze boot around my ankle. It was a relief when the enchanted metal went liquid again. Maybe it would turn back into a necklace. Maybe that would be the last attack on me for a while.

But as Grandma always said, if wishes were fishes, we'd all eat well tonight.

The liquid metal snaked up to my abdomen. It surrounded my middle, squeezing as it hardened. I pressed forward, fighting for breath, as I struggled to catch up to the hearse, the church members, and the dead who took up the rear.

I probably should have hid the body of the corpse I'd killed back there, but I didn't have time. Hopefully Dimitri would get it. Or Aimee. At least it was dead. As for the rest of them? They weren't attacking. That was a good thing.

I finally made it to the back of the procession.

One step at a time. My job was to figure out where they were going and why. I took refuge behind the crowd of the undead, lingering behind a straggler, a rotting woman with a twisted spine and half of her dress falling off. One hand hung limp while the other clawed toward the carriage winding its way up Royal Street.

We were moving toward the more crowded area of the French Quarter. We saw more cars, more people snapping pictures. They stood on the sidewalks and crossed the street behind me as the dead walked among them. What did they think this was? A parade?

Only in New Orleans.

I kept my head down and my feet moving. The one way I could figure that normal people could even see this when they couldn't see griffins or dragons or hear talking dogs was the fact that these corpses staggering up Royal were real people—just very, very dead.

And quite possibly bloodthirsty.

I'd come close to losing a chunk of my ankle back there and didn't even want to think about what would come of a bite. And I refused to even speak out loud what was now running through my mind—zombies.

We turned right on St. Peter and lost the crowd of onlookers as we passed next to the darkened park beyond.

Osse Pade still had the bug on him. The witches would be able to track him. And until backup arrived, it was up to me to keep control of this situation. Somehow. Only I had no idea what Mamma's end game could be, until I realized we were headed to St. Louis Cemetery Number One.

I heard movement behind me and nearly tripped when I saw a patch of grassy soil between the sidewalk and the street shaking as if there were something alive underneath.

Oh, no, no, no. I slowed. Stopped. Let out a gasp as a hand shot out of the soil.

I caught movement to my right and saw another corpse pulling itself out of the ground just inside the park.

Impossible.

But I knew better than that.

Still, what was that one doing in the park?

Then I remembered my history, how the yellow fever epidemic of 1793 had claimed a large part of the populace, and how they'd buried the corpses...everywhere.

Two more stumbled down the street from the right. Moaning.

Heaven almighty. I didn't understand how she could raise the dead, just passing by in her carriage. And worse, she drew to a stop in front of the gates of St. Louis Cemetery Number One.

This time, I didn't need to climb the tall white walls that surrounded the city of the dead. The gate opened on its own for Mamma Pade's carriage.

I took one more look back and saw Aimee in the street, clutching the arm of a man, most likely her husband. But they were too far back, and I didn't know what they could do at this point anyway. She'd be more help to Carpenter.

I pushed past the dead and followed Mamma inside. She stood on the main path, surrounded by mausoleums gleaming white under the light of the moon. "Where?"

Osse Pade led her to a crumbling tomb toward the back of the first row. "Andre is in here," he said, defeated.

Mamma cooed as she stroked the bokor's chin. He appeared almost happy then, until she reached out and laid a hand over her favorite son's final resting place.

"Rise up, my sweet Andre." She opened her arms. "That goes for all the departed who hear my call." She lifted her head and stretched her arms out. "If you wish to serve me, then you shall live again." She chuckled. "Do not worry. Never fear. All is well." She lowered her gaze and it landed square on me. "Mamma is here."

Rumbling filled the air, and I heard a sick scratching noise come from the tomb to my left. Someone was trying to get out.

A foot emerged from the soil in front of it, as if one of the dead had gotten turned around. Gray skin rubbed and tore against the white footpath as it tried to get a toehold.

I searched the sky for any sign of Dimitri. The scratching inside the tombs had grown more frantic. Louder.

Entire families were buried in these mausoleums, and if they were all coming back to life...I watched as the stone slab fell from the front of a tomb up ahead. A man stumbled out. Two more men and a woman toppled over him, followed by a child and another woman and, oh my word, in a minute we were going to have an unstoppable horde.

I couldn't kill this many. Even if I could, Mamma would raise more.

Osse Pade stood just beyond the melee. I stalked up to him and grabbed him by his cold, dead arm. "What the hell is your end game?"

He broke into a smile. "Mamma knows best," he said, latching onto me with inhuman strength.

Farther down, Mamma embraced a slack-jawed, blond-haired corpse with no nose or ears. "Andre baby," she said, ruffling his hair. She smiled at me, not even worried that I'd stop her.

I couldn't.

Not now, at least.

She let the blond corpse shuffle away. She stood at the center of the moaning undead and lowered her eyes.

Mamma began uttering incantations. Her human followers gathered around her, praying, lending their energy to her as she worked, asking for her blessings as more and more of the dead rose from their graves.

Her eyes snapped open and she smiled. "Now, my good people"—she reached down to them—"you will be transformed!"

They swayed and chanted, mesmerized as the dead surrounded them. I shouted a warning as a corpse drove its jaws into the neck of a woman in white. She arched forward, silently screaming. Blood sprayed as the zombie tore her throat out.

"Give yourselves! Surrender to death!" Mamma commanded the panicked crowd.

I broke away from Osse Pade and took down one corpse with a switch star. Two. I sliced their heads clean off. At least they couldn't bite. But the rest of the undead surged into the crowd, their fingers tearing, their jaws working.

It took no time for her to massacre them all. The bodies of the church members lay dead and bloody on the ground.

Mamma's eyes locked onto mine across the blood and the gore. "Don't worry. Mamma's here." She raised her arms, flung them wide, and I saw the bodies on the ground twitch. "You'll be better than you were before," she crooned to the grisly remains of her followers. "You'll be so much stronger." She grinned. "And you'll be mine."

Osse Pade gripped my arm. "It's beautiful, isn't it?" He pressed his lips against my neck with barely contained joy. "Once she has enough servants raised, she can draw the strength to bring you back from the dead."

Oh, hell no. "I'm not dead," I said, twisting in his grasp.

He kept hold of me and levered a knife at my heart. "You will be."

I broke free, wincing as his blade glanced off my bronze armor and sliced into the soft skin above. Hot pain seized me as I spun him around and grabbed his blade, holding him against me as I held it to his jugular.

Mamma jumped down from the tomb. "Kill him again." She laughed. She closed the distance between us. "Here. I'll do it for you." She took him by the neck and sliced him open with a sharp, bony finger. Blood sprayed as he fell to his knees.

I clutched a hand to my injured side. My vision swam. Frick, it hurt. I gathered my strength and focused on levitating. I needed to escape.

"No, no." Mamma gripped my shoulder and slammed me back to the ground. I'd only risen a few inches.

Osse Pade lay at our feet. I wasn't sure if he was alive or dead. "He's a good boy," she mused. "He tries. I don't know anyone else who has a demon-slayer minion."

"Not you," I ground out, even as I found myself surrounded by the dead.

Her jaws creaked as she smiled. "Yes, me." She brought a skeletal hand to my bleeding side and I could feel the pierce of her fingers as she worked her way inside my body. "Die, demon slayer."

CHAPTER TWENTY

Her cold fingers slithered inside me.

I slammed a switch star into her neck, taking her head clean off her shoulders. Blood splattered my face and I bent over in pain as I wrenched free of her grip.

Bodies pressed in on me from all sides, their dead hands holding me in place while Mamma snarled. Her head lay on the pavement several feet back, laughing at me.

It hurt to breathe. It hurt to think. I had to come up with something quick or I wasn't going to make it.

Spine twitching, Mamma held out her hand as a blood-soaked woman in white stumbled to retrieve her head with one good arm, the other gnarled and chewed away. Together, they placed the head back on Mamma's shoulders. She grimaced as she adjusted it back into place. Tendons slithered up the bone, muscles knit together, and I was left with a very alive, very pissed voodoo queen.

"I should kill you for that," she hissed. She adjusted a crick in her neck. "I will. But don't worry. I'll bring you back. You deserve to be my undead slave."

The ghouls held my arms out to my sides and shoved me toward Mamma.

"Disarm her!" Mamma commanded, more than a little put out.

At this point, I wouldn't be surprised if they ripped my arms off.

When the clawing dead bodies tore my switch star belt from my body, I was almost relieved. It disappeared into the churning mass of the departed.

"They should have done that back at the funeral parlor." She took one slow step toward me, then another. "My second son underestimated you. I won't."

She reached again for the hole in my chest, her fingers white and grasping.

I braced myself, knowing this time I might not make it.

"Lizzie!" My dog's voice echoed from above. I looked to the sky and saw Pirate swooping down on the back of his dragon. It was the most beautiful sight I'd ever seen. "Duck!" he hollered.

Flappy's talons hit Mamma, taking off her head, sending it screaming backward. The dead reached for the low-flying dragon.

I was loose.

Explosions lit up the night as spell jars broke all around us. The hoarse battle cry of the witches echoed over the city of the dead.

Red smoke rippled up, making my head swim. I stumbled sideways. I touched the wound at my side, horrified to see the blood running freely.

"Lizzie, catch!" Pirate yelled as Flappy came in for another dive. "It's from Dimitri." A loosely bound leather bag landed at my feet.

What the...? "Where's Dimitri?" I untied it to find a steel long sword.

"Attack!" Mamma ordered and I saw she had her head attached once more. "Kill. Rip her apart!"

The zombie horde surged. I hefted the sword and took off the heads of two of the creatures who came at me. The weapon slammed to the ground, heavier than I'd imagined.

Screams echoed in the night. I quickly climbed the nearest mausoleum, out of their reach. For now. I sliced at the hands grabbing for me. The Red Skulls had invaded from the front gate. They'd made it about twenty feet inside the cemetery and set up a preliminary circle.

A wall of green magic surrounded them, and they hunkered behind it, firing red Death spells. Trunks lay open along the edges and in the center of the circle, filled with glistening magic.

I'd seen Death spells before. Hell, I was the only person alive who had walked through one and not succumbed. But that brand of magic didn't work now. Not on these creatures.

"Bob!" I hollered, trying to get the nearest Red Skull's attention.

Moans filled the night as the witches were quickly surrounded.

Ant Eater and Grandma barked orders to the coven members passing spells up to the front.

A corpse's jagged teeth lashed at my ankle. I sliced its head off.

"They're already dead!" I hollered as the bloodthirsty corpses slammed into their lines and reached for me on top of the mausoleum. The zombies pressed against the Red Skull's wall, pushing and straining.

An arm reached through, then another, trying to grasp at the witches beyond. The spell powering the wall weakened and sputtered. It wouldn't hold for long.

On the right flank, Dimitri defended his position with a short sword. He'd found a pair of black pants, but that's all he wore. The muscles in his back flexed as he drove back the dead again and again. Creely lay next to him, white-faced, her side bleeding. Edwina frantically applied bandages.

The dead were starting to pile up, to push over the wall. A hand shot through and grabbed Dimitri's shoulder. He sliced it right off the arm. But there would be others. Countless many more.

A snarling corpse seized my leg and I lopped off its head moments before it bit.

With gut-wrenching terror, I saw the first of the dead break through the witches' wall and go straight for Dimitri. He stabbed it in the head, then dropped his blade. He had to be nuts.

I watched as he wove his blue protective magic, patching the hole. At least temporarily. Dimitri's arms shook. He focused his entire body, his entire being on that breach in the wall. He was working too hard to keep it closed. It was only a matter of time.

Ant Eater rushed for more weapons, splitting them with Aimee and her man as they went back to the walls. I hoped to God they had more in their arsenal. We had to end this or all of us would die tonight.

I shoved off the tomb, levitating over the bloodthirsty corpses, landing hard inside the witches' barricade. I ran for Grandma as she dragged a teetering zombie over the wall and stabbed it in the brain with a dagger.

Its dull eyes closed forever and she gave a satisfied snort.

Yeah, well, there were too many to kill one-on-one. "We have to come up with something bigger," I hollered over the snarls coming from outside the wall. "You can't use Death spells on the already dead."

"Right," she said, her eyes widening. She hurried to the stash at the center and began rifling through it. "We've got stuff to stop a heart."

"No."

"Turn blood to dust."

"No," I insisted. "What do you have that can short-circuit a brain?" Maybe the zombie movies had gotten something right.

"I got Mind Wipers," she said, a little desperate.

"No." Not when their ultimate wish was to tear us apart.

The shambling corpses pressed into the wall and I heard it crackle under the pressure.

"What have you got to kill them?" I demanded.

"Everything we've got is designed to kill them!" she hollered back.

It was just that none of it would work on corpses. *Think.*

I jumped sideways when Frieda pressed a crystal over the bloody gash on my side. "Ow!" I slapped her away.

She pressed it in harder. "Stop being a baby. You won't be any good to us if you bleed to death."

"I'm fine." I grimaced as I felt warm magic seep into my wound. Damn. It stung.

"Hold still," she ordered.

Flappy circled overhead and shot down straight toward me, with a wobbling Pirate on his back. The damned dog was going to fall off one of these days. I didn't know how many times I told him *not* to ride the dragon.

"Get away!" I yelled, waving him off. He was flying straight over Death spells.

He didn't listen. The fricking dog never listened. He skimmed the wall, taking down a mess of zombies as they bit and clawed at Flappy's legs.

The dragon shot out a burst of fire, setting several of the dead ablaze. Fire crackled over their skin and clothes. It streamed from their hair. The stench of burning, rotting flesh invaded my senses and still they came at us, arms outstretched.

Frieda rushed to help Ant Eater, whose boot had caught fire.

Next to her, Aimee staggered back from the wall. For a second I thought she'd been bitten. "We can't fight this," she said, blood flowing from a cut on her forehead. "You have to kill Mamma."

"I tried to kill Mamma," I countered. "I ripped out her soul. I stabbed her in the head. She's immortal."

"No." She grabbed my arm violently as a wave of red smoke shot up nearby. Way too close. "You have to kill her *in her grave!*"

I stared at her. "You sure?"

She held my gaze. "Positive."

"Good Lord." I hoped she was right.

I climbed up on top of a trunk near the wall, unsure how I could even pull it off. If this worked, if I could make it there, this could be our salvation.

I'd have to levitate and then make a run for it.

Meanwhile, I sliced the arms off an old man who was about to take a chunk out of Flappy's leg.

Flappy took off, jolting up into the sky.

"You can do it!" My dog's voice floated down to me.

He was in so much trouble right now.

But first I had to find the immortal voodoo queen. And lead her to her grave. And kill her.

I bashed in the skull of a creature who was more bone than anything, and leapt out of the circle, landing on the roof of a brick grave that crumbled under my feet. The red smoke from the Death spells stung my eyes, making them water. My side felt raw, but most of the bleeding had stopped. Go, Frieda.

"You want me?" I hollered to the voodoo queen. "Come get me."

I saw her advance through the mess of bodies and I did something I'd never done before. I ran away.

Jumping down off the far side of the grave, I took off like a shot, toward the rear left side of the cemetery. My boots pounded against the packed ground as I ran over the seashell paths and through the uneven graves. I found a relatively deserted path and took down a dead bride on the way up to the white stone lane where I hoped and prayed I'd find the Pade family tomb.

A wave of screams erupted behind me. I had to believe Dimitri and the witches were holding their own. That it was a battle cry, not the sound of my friends being ripped apart.

The whispers of the dead followed me. Their spirits tangled in my hair, chilling me to the core. They wound in front of me, misty and white.

I tore straight through them.

And then I saw it, the Pade grave straight ahead, on the dead end. It stood plain and white, topped with a slanted roof, the entrance flanked by vases of crimson roses twined with strands of pearls and feathers. More flowers were scattered on the ground in front of the entrance, along with offerings of rum and cigarettes.

I stomped them in my haste.

The tomb was cursed. I would be too in a minute. I spread my hands over the freezing cold stone, even as I sweated in the heat of the night. I found the lever, slid it to the side and stood back as the stone rolled away.

Dark energy tore at my skin and I remembered Aimee's warning. It could very well kill me to proceed, but dammit, I was about to make sure it was positively lethal for Mamma Pade.

"Sacrifice yourself." It was one of the three Truths of the demon slayers and I clung to it now.

A dead hand landed heavy on my shoulder and I gasped. I spun and came up hard against a very strong, very angry Mamma.

This time, she stood alone, away from her ghouls and her henchmen.

"I'm not going in there and neither are you," she hissed.

I grabbed her hand and fell back into the tomb.

Icy coldness washed over me and I let out a cry as my head slammed against the floor. I had to stay conscious, keep hold of the sword, even as Mamma's corpse crashed down on top of me.

I'd lost most of the feeling in my arms. I didn't even know if I could swing the heavy sword as Mamma rose up, her fingers closing around my neck.

I stabbed her in the chest, the sword going in hard, catching on bone. It drove her off my neck, but it didn't kill her. If anything, it ticked her off.

She snarled, working her body on the sword until I realized she was impaling herself to get to me.

I braced a foot on her chest and fought her, using every bit of strength I had left to dislodge her body from my weapon. My head swam. The wound on my side throbbed, trickling warm blood against my cold skin as Mamma's bony fingers found my throat once more.

My fingers weakened their grip. I couldn't feel them anymore. I had to find my strength somehow. Had to fight.

I thought of Dimitri and the witches, surrounded, fighting a losing battle against the horde. I thought of Pirate and what would happen to him if everyone he loved were gone. I thought of what I had with Dimitri and how I refused to lose that over a crazed voodoo bokor and his damned mother.

So I shoved both my feet against her chest and yanked the sword back and kicked her into the ceiling. She slammed against the stone. I rolled away as she fell back down. And once she landed, I rose to my knees and sliced her sick, smiling skull in half for good.

The black soul burst from her throat, breaking into hundreds of tiny shards that flew straight at me. I shielded my face and closed my eyes as they seared past me and out into the night.

Free.

Chapter Twenty-One

Mamma's bones rested on the dirt-caked floor of her grave. As it should be.

I watched the light fade from her eyes. The flesh flaked and crumbled from her bones. Her eyeballs sank into her skull and returned to dust. And when I was satisfied that she lay well and truly dead, I stepped out of the grave.

The moans of the dead echoed throughout the darkened cemetery.

A young blonde girl stumbled toward me. She couldn't have been more than ten. Blood trailed from her mouth, but at the moment, she appeared more stunned than deadly.

"I've got her," said a gristly voice on my right.

Carpenter stepped out from between the graves, flanked by Frieda and Aimee. A white bandage wrapped his chest. He looked like he'd seen better days, but he was whole and alive.

Thank God.

He stretched a hand out to her and she jolted to attention. "This way, sweetheart," he said, ushering her toward an open mausoleum a few graves down. Her tiny feet scraped the dirt as she shuffled back to her place of rest.

"Now this one," Carpenter said, turning weakly to beckon a pale and confused Osse Pade. Without Mamma, he'd lost his intellect, his awareness. "Go," Carpenter said, pointing to the grave of the Three Sisters. I stepped aside and let the bokor enter.

"Don't let anyone else near this place," I warned, "it's cursed." I sure felt like death warmed over.

The necromancer shook his head. "That curse died with Mamma." He paused. "You did kill her, didn't you?"

Way to take it for granted. "Yes," I said, trying to sound cocky, even as I admitted my failing. "Her soul went free."

Carpenter squinted and looked to the sky, as if he could somehow see it. "It was free before."

I didn't even want to think about it.

"How are you feeling?" I asked.

He shrugged. "About as bad as you look," he said, his attention returning to me.

"He was too busy destroying records to worry about bleeding to death," Aimee said, tears clouding her eyes. "Frieda got to him just in time."

The biker witch shrugged, embarrassed. "We all do what we can."

"We figured out how to stop Mamma," Carpenter said, as if that was all that mattered. "And I made it so the secret to Osse Pade's soul traps died with him."

Dimitri stepped from between the graves. Sweat shone on his body. His hair was a mess and blood marred his cheek, but he was whole and alive.

"Lizzie," he said, scooping me up, kissing me for all I was worth. I ignored the groans of the rest and let him. I only had one love, one person I woke up for in the morning and thought about every night before I went to sleep. And he was here now. Whole and healthy.

Life had never been so sweet.

†††

We helped the witches clean up while Carpenter returned the cemetery dead to their graves.

"What do we do about the rest?" Ant Eater asked Grandma.

We'd laid out the church members in neat rows and covered their faces as best we could with the white cloths the witches had used to wrap spells inside the trunks.

Grandma shook her head. "I don't know. It's a shame."

"They should have stayed off the dark path," said the man whom I'd seen with Aimee earlier. He had a Spanish accent and was quite the looker in an Antonio Banderas sort of way. He held out a hand to me. "Dante Montenegro, Aimee's husband."

"What a way to meet you," I said, taking his hand.

He nodded to Dimitri, who merely smiled. Evidently, I'd missed out on a joke.

"Do you deal with this sort of thing a lot?" I asked Dante, trying to figure out what was going on.

"The dead coming back to life?" He laughed. "Not often," he mused, shooting Dimitri a look. Let them have their little secret. "I must say, though, my brother-in-law does attract trouble."

I didn't doubt it. "He's one of the best I know." He'd sacrificed himself to try to stop Osse Pade and to keep the witches and me safe. And even though he'd gotten us into this mess in the first place, he did it for the right reasons. "We all owe him a debt."

"I heard that," Carpenter said behind me.

Dimitri groaned.

"No," I said, "he's not going to hold me to that one."

Carpenter merely smiled.

Before we left the cemetery, we closed up the graves and Aimee sealed the tomb of the Three Sisters with magic that made my hair sizzle. Even the biker witches broke out into applause, although to be fair, they'd also found a flask of cinnamon schnapps among the spell jars and had laid into it pretty heavy by the time we were ready to go.

We'd all survived the battle, and that was something to celebrate.

Even Creely partook, which I thought was a bit much, given her age and her injury...until Frieda showed me her work. The gash in the engineering witch's side had closed up completely, leaving a pink line of irritated flesh. I lifted my shirt and found nearly the same thing.

"You've got a natural talent for this," I told the blonde witch. We'd lost our healer a few months before, in a battle with a demon. "You ever think you might want to take on the job for good?"

She blushed and shook her head, her hoop earrings swinging. "Oh, I don't know."

I did. "Think about it."

Life's too short to try to hide your talents.

Chapter Twenty-Two

News outlets reported the next day about Osse Pade's voodoo church, and how all of the members had committed mass suicide.

Aimee hadn't been happy. It was bad PR for a religion that could be quite beautiful in the right hands. But, frankly, I was just glad to be getting out of town.

I missed our home. The trip to New Orleans had taken longer than we'd expected. My first wedding anniversary was coming up in a few days and I wanted to focus on love and happiness, not curses and death.

We gathered outside Grand-mère Chantal's house, packing up the bus. Dimitri stopped to give me a kiss before helping the witches haul a spell trunk onto the waiting bus. We'd used all of the extra spells to brighten up the house, which was good, because I could swear I saw the wall in the front room getting a little bloody on top.

We'd been houseguests long enough. The ghosts could roam free again and hopefully find some added peace. I wished it for all of them, even the spirit in the séance room.

"I took the restraining spell off," Ant Eater said as she followed my gaze up to the tower.

"What was that thing?" It had been right about so much—about the evil we faced, about the blood and the bones. It hadn't asked for anything in return. My attention, maybe, but nothing else.

Ant Eater shrugged. "I guess we'll never know."

She might be happy with that, but I wasn't.

We still had a few minutes before everything made it out to the busses and the bikes. I slipped back inside and climbed the stairs. I edged down the hallway and entered the door that led up to the tower.

There was no harm in it anymore. I was leaving. It had to stay.

I took the final set of stairs quickly and slowed only a hair when the gold door creaked open without me touching it.

"Glad I'm not interrupting," I said as I stepped into the old séance room. It appeared the same as before. Dark, with gritty windows, extravagant wallpaper, and the circular wood table at the center. I looked to the Ouija board that had greeted me before.

But this time, I heard the voice instead, the one from my dream. "You missed something." It echoed in the small space, low and smug.

I didn't take the bait. "Tell me. How did you know how to defeat the voodoo queen?"

He chuckled low, and I felt it in my gut. "I know...so much."

Maybe it hadn't been such a great idea to return.

The Ouija board remained motionless. The air in the room hung heavy. "Okay, I'm leaving now." I turned toward the door.

"You can try."

I'd do more than that. I closed the door behind me and didn't look back.

✝✝✝

Dimitri stood in the bright sunshine, along with Pirate and Flappy. "I told Pirate he could ride the dragon back," my husband said, "at least until we stop for lunch."

"I'm trying to *dis*courage him," I said as Pirate yipped with joy and the dragon danced.

"They've proven they can be responsible," Dimitri countered, as if saving my skin in an undead cemetery battle counted.

"Oh, all right," I said, letting my husband wrap his arms around me.

"You realize this will keep them busy," he murmured against the soft, sensitive skin near my ear.

"Well, when you put it that way..." I brushed a kiss across his cheek.

A few of the Red Skulls whistled at us, but I didn't care.

I climbed on my bike next to Dimitri and watched Ant Eater lock the door to the house, hopefully for good.

"You ready?" Dimitri asked, drawing his helmet on.

"Always," I said, doing the same. We were whole, free, and ready for whatever adventures lay down the road. Life was good, and I intended to savor every minute of it.

~THE END~

Author's Note:

The Accidental Demon Slayer series began on the back of a Macy's envelope. I'd been up all night with my infant son and while I was walking him around, I had this idea about a demon slayer and a gang of biker witches. The book was a complete joy to write and it became my first published novel.

Thank you for sharing this journey with me and for reading. I'm excited to report there will be at least three more books in the series. If you'd like to receive an email each time I release a new book, sign up at www.angiefoxcom. And because you deserve a special treat, I give out ten free advanced reading copies of the next book in each email. Be sure to check for your name on the winner's list.

Wishing you all the best!
Angie

Available now!
Southern Spirits
Southern Ghost Hunter Mysteries, Book #1
By Angie Fox

When out of work graphic designer Verity Long accidentally traps a ghost on her property, she's saddled with more than a supernatural sidekick—she gains the ability see spirits. It leads to an offer she can't refuse from the town's bad boy, the brother of her ex and the last man she should ever partner with.

Ellis Wyatt is in possession of a stunning historic property haunted by some of Sugarland Tennessee's finest former citizens. Only some of them are growing restless—and destructive. He hires Verity to put an end to the disturbances. But soon, Verity learns there's more to the mysterious estate than floating specters, secret passageways, and hidden rooms.

There's a modern day mystery afoot, one that hinges on a decades-old murder. Verity isn't above questioning the living, or the dead. But can she discover the truth before the killer finds her?

An Excerpt from
Southern Spirits

Chapter One

I lived in a gorgeous antebellum house. Not too large. Certainly not too small. The white columns out front were tasteful, even though they had chipped in places. The porch was welcoming, if a little weathered. Over the years, my family had sold the estate around the house, piece by piece, so that the sprawling peach orchard and even the grand front drive had given way to tidy bungalows lining the long road to the main house.

Grandma had said it made gossip travel even faster, the way they built houses so close together these days. I always told her that the good citizens of Sugarland, Tennessee needed no help.

Still, I loved the place.

And I absolutely despised letting it go.

"Anyone home?" my best friend Lauralee called from the front of the house. "Verity, are you in here?" She added a few knocks on the front door, out of politeness rather than practicality, since the door already stood open.

We'd endured a stifling hot afternoon, and I couldn't afford to run the air conditioning. I needed any breeze I could get.

"In the back parlor," I called. "Mourning," I added, since there was nothing left in the once-stately room, save for a cooler filled with ice, my tea jug, and a lopsided futon I inherited from a roommate back at Ole Miss. The pink-papered walls and elegant wood accents appeared so strange without rugs and furniture, like a queen stripped of her jewels.

The estate sale was yesterday and the place had been picked clean. The vultures.

"I'm sorry." Lauralee's voice echoed in the empty room. She let her purse and a cloth grocery sack slip from her shoulder to the floor, then she wrapped an arm around me and squeezed, the curled end of her ponytail tickling my cheek.

I gazed up at the ugly black hole where the crystal chandelier had hung for more than one hundred years. "Thanks." I'd come to terms with this. I really had. I turned and looked her straight in the baby blues. "I'd live in a paper bag if it meant I didn't have to marry that bastard."

My friend drew back and tucked a lock of my hair behind my ear. "Seems like he's trying to make you good on your word."

"True. But I'm not done yet." I refused to even entertain the thought.

This past May, I'd scandalized the town when I jilted the most eligible bachelor in three counties—at the altar, no less. It was a disaster. Two old ladies fainted straight out of the pew reserved for the Southern Heritage Club. Then Beau's own mother collapsed, taking down a lovely hydrangea arrangement. I secretly wondered if Mrs. Leland Herworth Wydell III didn't want to be upstaged, even at her own son's ultimate humiliation.

Truth was, he'd brought it upon himself. But I suppose it was quite shocking if you didn't know the details.

I hadn't told a lot of people. I'd wanted to spare my sister.

Lauralee chewed on her lip as she surveyed what little remained in my home. "Tell me you at least made some decent money yesterday."

"I did." I'd sold everything I could lay my hands on and kept only the absolute necessities, namely my futon, my grandmother's pearl wedding ring, and the quilts she'd made for me. It had hurt like a physical pain. I'd had to remind myself that it was only furniture, clothes. *Stuff.* I still had my health. And my friends. Not to mention my family. I brought a hand to my throat, where I used to wear my grandmother's cross from when she was about my age. The delicate gold and silver filigree antique now belonged to my not-quite-mother-in-law. "I still owe more than twenty thousand dollars."

I gazed across the once-grand, now empty back parlor turned family room. I tried to ignore the hollow place in my stomach. Tomorrow, my ancestral home would go on the market. I let out a ragged sigh. "It's dumb, but I keep hoping for a miracle."

A hidden treasure in the attic. Gold under the stairs. Stranger things had happened, right? All I knew was that I couldn't lose this house. I just couldn't.

Lauralee wrapped an arm around my shoulder and gave me a squeeze. "You'll make it. You always do," she said, in a way that made me think she actually believed it. She took in the fourteen-foot ceilings, the crown moldings. "With the money you have left over from the sale, you can make a fresh go of things."

A new start. I certainly needed *something* to change. And yet...

"I can't believe it's all gone." What had taken more than a century to accumulate had become fractured history in the space of a day. "Except for that," I said, pointing to a godawful vase on the mantel.

My friend made a face. "I never even noticed that before."

It would have been hard to ignore. "It was in the attic," I explained. "Where it belongs." The green stones that circled the top were sort of pretty, but a crude, hand-painted scene marred the copper exterior and a healthy dent gouged the lower half. The dotty old relic looked completely out of place on an ornate marble mantel with flowers and hummingbirds carved into the corners.

"Yeek." Lauralee crossed the room for a better look. She attempted to lift the monstrosity, and then changed her mind. It was heavier than it looked, wider at the top and tapered down to a flared base at the bottom. In fact, it reminded me more of an antique Grecian urn. She turned to me. "Is it a spittoon?"

"I think it's a vase," I said, joining her. "Beau gave it to me. He called it an historic heirloom. Looking back, I think he just needed to get rid of it."

In the beginning of our relationship, Beau had given me heartfelt gifts—a pressed flower from the picnic we took on our first date, a little notebook with one of our private jokes written on the inside cover. Later, it was last-minute gas station flowers.

And objects like this.

"It's hideous," Lauralee said.

"A true monstrosity," I agreed. Or else he would have let me return it when I gave him back the ring. "You want it?" I asked, turning the dented side toward her.

My friend let out a snort. "Not unless I can thunk your ex over the head with it."

I shot her a conspiratorial grin. "You'd do that for me?"

She raised her delicate brows. "Nothing would give me more pleasure," she said in a sweet, southern tone that would make you think I'd offered mint juleps on the verandah.

"I suppose I could toss it," I said. I still had one trash can left.

She waved me off. "Keep it out. It's a focal piece. The only one you have. Here." She scooted it over toward the pale shadow where my mother's crystal swan used to be. "It'll draw people's eyes to the fireplace instead of that hideous futon."

"Way to remind me that I'm sleeping in the parlor." No way was I going to try dragging a futon up a flight of stairs.

She crossed over to the opposite wall to retrieve her

hemp grocery bag from the floor. "Maybe this will help you forget," she said, holding up a bottle of Malbec.

"Mine," I said, on her in an instant. Although I'd have to tell her Beau took the stemware.

She handed me the bottle and the opener, then pulled out a pair of plastic wine glass tops from her bag. "My kids used the bottoms to play flying saucer frisbee, but I didn't think you'd mind."

I wound the opener into the cork. "Who won?"

"Who knows?" She held out both glasses and I poured.

It was well past cocktail hour in the old south. In fact, the sun was beginning to set.

"Should we retire to the floor?" I asked, a bit punchy with the unreality of it all.

Lauralee handed me a glass. "We might end up there anyway," she said as we both took a seat.

I smelled lemon polish and old wood as I stretched my legs out over the floor I'd lovingly scrubbed. We leaned our backs against the plaster wall and sipped our wine as the shadows lengthened over the room.

It's not like I had any lamps.

"You ever think what might have happened if I hadn't come back home?" I asked her.

I could have gone to the big city after graduating art school. My father died when I was in fifth grade, my mother long since remarried. My sister had bounced around from college to college. I could have found a job at an advertising firm, or at a large company with an in-house graphics department. I wouldn't have been around when Beauregard Buford Wydell decided it was time to take a wife.

This place would have sat empty, but at least it would have stayed mine.

"You belong here, Verity," she said simply, as if it were the only truth.

She had me pegged. I cherished this town and my home. There'd been no other choice for me. Without my roots and my family's heritage, I'd be adrift.

Grandma knew. It was why she left the house to me when she died. The rest of the estate went to my mother, who bought an RV and embraced adventure with my stepfather; and to my sister, who used her portion to pay for her various semesters abroad and half-finished degrees.

But, truly, this place had been mine even before Grandma made it legal.

I took an extra large sip of wine as Lauralee's phone chimed. She handed me her glass and pulled the smart phone from her back pocket. The glowing screen lit her pixie face and what she saw made her frown.

"Trouble in paradise?" I asked as she checked her text messages.

The faint lines around her eyes crinkled at the corners and she sighed. "It's Big Tom. Tommy Junior got his head stuck in the hallway banister again."

I should have faked some sympathy, but it happened at least once a month. The kid was forever getting stuck in something. "Do you have to leave?"

"No." She took her wine back from me. "Big Tom has it handled." She held her glass like a diva at a cocktail party. "Heck, if I was home, I'd be calling him. He's better at prying the railings off."

I tried to imagine it and failed. "I'm starting to think you need the wine more than I do." She had four children under the age of seven—all boys.

She gave me the old pish-posh as she leaned against the wall. "It's the first two kids that get you. After that, you're broken in."

I'd take her word for it.

A beam of slanting sunlight caught the ugly vase and shone through the dust in the air around it in a way that reminded me of dozens of mini fireflies. The copper itself didn't gleam a bit.

"Oh my God..." Lauralee, said, leaning forward, glass in hand. "It's dirty," she said with relish.

"I saw the dust," I told her. I'd give it a good scrubbing before the open house tomorrow.

But she was already halfway to her feet. "No. The painting on it is dirty. As in sexy time."

"No way," I said, practically leaping off the floor to get a look.

"It's so bad it's brilliant," she laughed, as I pulled the vase from the mantel. "I don't know why I didn't notice it before. Now that I see it, I can't *not* see it."

"Where?" I asked. Yes, there were some highly styled, almost art-deco swirly bits. They were hard to make out. It looked like people dancing. Maybe.

My friend rolled her eyes. "Has it been that long since you got laid?"

"I plead the fifth," I said, as I carried the vase over to a beam of fading sunlight by the window. I traced a finger over the crude painting. Then I saw it—a girl, and a boy...and another boy. Now how did that work?

"They're getting lucky," Lauralee said, crowding me to get another look. "It's a lucky vase."

I stifled a snicker. "Can you see Beau's mother displaying this in her parlor? Maybe she knows what the girl is doing with two boys."

"And I think there's a goat," Lauralee added.

"No." I said, yanking it closer to see.

"Made you look," she laughed.

Did she ever.

"Wait till the old biddies see this," I said. And they would. We'd have plenty of gawkers tomorrow.

Lauralee gave me a loving punch to the arm. "You might have to point it out to them. They'll gasp and moan but they'll secretly love it."

My friend's phone chimed again. She looked, and this time her sigh was heavier. "Rats."

"Trouble?"

She held up her phone to show me a text photo of her five-year-old son, sitting next to a pile of debris, grinning.

"Hiram got hold of a screwdriver and took apart the hall clock while Tom was working on the banister. I'd better go."

Typical day in the Clementine household. I folded her into a hug. "Thanks for the support."

She squeezed hard. "Thanks for the laugh." She smiled as she pulled back. "I love you, girlie." She tilted her chin down. "And I, for one, am glad you came home."

She was a true friend, and for that I was grateful. "Me, too."

†††

After she left, I took that vase off the mantel and traced my finger over it. Boy, girl…and that really could be a goat. I smiled to myself. Lauralee was right. I would make it through this, despite Beau and his mother and every damned one of them.

I'd be strong. Free. Maybe not quite as free as those happy fun time people painted on the vase, but I'd be a new woman all the same. My own woman.

I wet the pad of my thumb and used it to wipe the dust from the rim. As I did, something shifted inside of it. Strange. I lifted the small bronze lid and saw at least three inches of dirt.

Well, no wonder. Nobody had cleaned the thing or showed it any love in ages.

No problem. I'd take it outside and rinse it down with the hose. I could turn the dented spot toward the wall and this little piece of faded glory might pass for something worth buying.

Now would also be a good time to track down Lucy. That sneaky little skunk would spend all night outside terrorizing the neighbors if I'd let her.

I pushed past the screen door and saw she wasn't in her bed out on our sprawling back porch. A walk down the steps showed she wasn't under her favorite apple tree, either—or as she probably thought of it: the place where snacks dropped down from heaven. After a little bit of searching, I found Lucy catching the last bit of sun on the stone pavers lining the rose garden at the back of the house.

As soon as she saw me, she rolled right off the paver and landed on her back in the grass. She gave a chipper, skunky grunt and waddled over to greet me. I loved the way she walked, with her head down and her little body churning with every step. It was the cutest thing ever.

"Hiya, sweetie pie," I bent down on one knee to greet her. She thrust her entire snout into my palm and then turned her head for easy petting, making husky, purr-like squawks. She had the softest little cheeks. I stroked her there, then down along the neck and between the ears in the way that made her right back leg twitch. "You enjoying your last day at the house?"

An apartment just wasn't going to be the same for Lucy. I'd found a place that accepted exotic pets, but believe it or not, people around here held a certain bias against skunks. It wasn't enough that I'd had little Lucy's scent glands removed. They wanted her to stop being who she was.

Poor baby.

I'd have to make some adjustments as well after we moved. Our new home, The Regal Towers, was basically an old six-family flat down by the railroad tracks. So close, in fact, that the windows rattled every time a train went by. The doors were made of plywood. I wasn't even sure that was legal, not that management cared. Morton Davis, slumlord extraordinaire, had offered to save it for me on account of the fact we'd attended grades K through eight together at Stonewall Jackson Elementary. I knew it was available because no one else wanted it.

There had to be a way out of this.

Lucy snuggled up to me and tried to climb my leg to get closer.

"You want to help?" I asked making sure I reached clear of Lucy as I dumped the contents of the vase over Grandma's rose bushes. She gave the little pile a sniff and sneezed.

"You said it." The dirt was loose and dry, which I was glad to see. I'd heard that sort of thing was good for the roots.

It certainly couldn't hurt.

When the last of the fine dust had settled down out of the air, I hosed out the vase and poured the water on the roses. They needed it. I'd been neglecting them lately.

"How do you like that?" I asked my climbing vines.

A chilly breeze whipped straight up my spine and shot goose bumps down my arms. It startled me, and I dropped the vase. Lucy darted away.

"Nice work, butterfingers," I mumbled to myself, retrieving it. I spotted a stubborn patch of dirt down in the base and rinsed it out again, but the stuff wouldn't budge.

The rose bushes shuddered. It had to be the wind, but this time, I didn't feel it.

For the first time, I felt uncomfortable in my grandmother's garden.

It was a strange feeling, and an unwelcome one at that. "It's getting late," I told myself, as if that would explain it.

Quick as I could, I reached for the rose snippers I kept under the hose. I cut a full red bloom, with a stem as thick as my finger, and popped it into the vase with a dash of water. Then I hurried back toward the house, careful not to spill a drop.

"Lucy," I called, half-wondering if the skunk wasn't the source of the strange rustling in the rose bushes behind me. "Come on, girl."

She came running from her hiding place under the porch. Something had scared her, too.

The house had never been what you'd call ordinary. We had fish in the pond, each one big as a cat; more often than not, I found fireflies in the attic.

But this was unusual, even for my ancestral home. I didn't like it at all.

Especially when the windows rattled.

"What the hey, girl?" I asked Lucy. And myself.

She turned around and headed back under the porch. Darn it all. She tended to snuggle under my covers at night and I didn't want her all dirty.

You have no idea how hard it is to give a skunk a bath.

A low creaking came from inside the house. The hair on my arms stood on end. Perhaps Lucy was the smart one after all. Unfortunately, there wasn't room under the porch for me.

Instead, I took the steps slowly and crossed the threshold into the darkened kitchen.

My eyes strained against the shadows. Not for the first time, I wished I'd kept at least one light. With shaking fingers, I lit the big, orange, three-wicked candle I'd been using for the last few days.

The house stood still, quiet as a grave. Almost as if it were waiting.

"Is it you, Grandma?" I asked on a whisper. "Are you mad I'm selling?"

If she'd been watching down on me at all—and I knew she did—Grandma would understand I'd been given no choice in the matter.

"Oh no," said a ghostly male voice. "You're staying put, sweetheart." With shock and horror, I realized it was coming from the vase. I dropped it.

The door slammed closed behind me. The bolt clicked, locking on its own as the vase spun and rattled to a stop on the floor.

A chill swept the room. I retreated until my back hit solid wood. I'd never seen a ghost or heard a ghost although I watched Ghost Adventures on television and I certainly believed in them and sweet Jesus I was trapped.

I couldn't feel my fingers, or my limbs for that matter. My entire body had gone ice cold. "What do you want?" I asked, voice shaking. Seeing as I hadn't dropped dead on the spot from a heart attack, this had better well be my salvation. "Why are you here?"

The voice laughed, as if it were honest-to-God amused. "I'm here because you chiseled me, princess."

SOUTHERN SPIRITS
First in a new series by Angie Fox
Available Now!

ABOUT THE AUTHOR

Angie Fox is the *New York Times* bestselling author of several books about vampires, werewolves and things that go bump in the night. She claims that researching her stories can be just as much fun as writing them. In the name of fact-finding, Angie has ridden with Harley biker gangs, explored the tunnels underneath Hoover Dam and found an interesting recipe for Mamma Coalpot's Southern Skunk Surprise (she's still trying to get her courage up to try it).

Angie earned a Journalism degree from the University of Missouri. During that time, she also skipped class for an entire week so she could read Anne Rice's vampire series straight through. Angie has always loved books and is shocked, honored and tickled pink that she now gets to write books for a living. Although, she did skip writing for a few weeks last year so she could read Lynsay Sands Argeneau vampire series straight through.

Angie makes her home in St. Louis, Missouri with a football-addicted husband, two kids, and Moxie the dog.

If you want to receive an email reminder the next time Angie releases a new book, sign up at **www.angiefox.com**.